TALES OF A THE LITTLEST MERMAID

LOU WILHAM

Midnight Tide
PUBLISHING

Also by Lou Wilham

The Curse Collection
    The Curse of The Black Cat
    The Curse of Ash and Blood

The Sea Witch Trilogy
    Tales of the Sea Witch
    Tales of the Littlest Mermaid

The Clockwork Chronicles
    The Girl in the Clockwork Tower
    The Unicorn and the Clockwork Quest

Villainous Heroics
    Villainous

The Heir to Moondust
    The Prince of Starlight

The Medusa Project

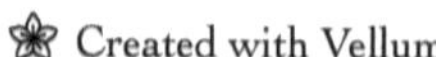 Created with Vellum

For Lissa & Val,
who gave me the courage to
build worlds from words.

Tales of the Littlest Mermaid

A LITTLE MERMAID RETELLING

Prologue

ords have power.

Some more than others.

Then there are names, which can inspire hope or strike terror into one's heart. The name Irsa was the latter.

The Witch of the Deep's name had long been reviled and feared by the people of Alon for her widespread feud with their king. No one is quite sure how it began. What they are sure of is that the hatred between the pair now threatened to swallow Alon with its darkness.

This is the story of how Irsa of Tjena lost her name.

ONE

Irsa

---

*I*rsa was losing *her*, little by little. It had started with her name, had expanded to her voice, then how many freckles she'd had, and soon it would be the color of her eyes or her smile.

Everything had a price, and that was the bargain Irsa had struck with the dark writhing powers of the depths of the ocean. Her memories for the ability to bring Tynan to bent tail. Funny how she could remember his name but had lost the name of the one she was doing this for. Not that it mattered much. Irsa was sure before this was done, she'd have no memories left at all.

"Still, it stands," she seethed, her nails digging crescents into the soft flesh of her palms. "I've lost so much and still, it stands!"

Tynan had built a magical barrier around the city of Alon, leaving the rest of his kingdom to fend for itself in a foolhardy bid to protect himself and his children. She'd picked off the outlying towns and villages that fell under Tynan's rule one by one, leveling the buildings, killing anyone who dared linger, leaving only the city around the castle overflowing now with refugees from Irsa and Tynan's war. They had been easy prey for her to test her newfound powers on in the early years of their feud. But how stupid he was to think that Irsa had ever cared about them. All she cared about was the turquoise-headed mer who had stolen her love from her. She'd make him pay.

"It is weakening, Mistress," a soft voice slithered across her mind from where the sea dragon bobbed beside her. It was eerie having a mental link to the dark creatures of the depths. Their minds were strange and twisted, full of writhing shadows that, if she looked too closely, would swallow her whole, making their motivations that much harder to parse. "It will not be much longer."

"There has to be more we can do." Irsa's fingers drummed on her bent tail. "All these curses and plagues. They're good. But they're punishing more than Tynan, aren't they?" She let out a breath. "I've got so much blood on my hands these days."

"They would be happy if you were dead, Mistress. Just as the king would."

"Yes, well, whose fault is that?!" Like the electric strike of an eel, Irsa's rage flashed to life, lighting up the dark outcropping of rocks they'd perched themselves on. "Whose fault is it that they hate me?!"

The little sea dragon merely looked up at her with its bottomless black eyes. Darker than the pit where they'd buried her love some eighteen years ago. One would think she'd have gotten used to the way these beasts looked at her with their empty eyes, and their spindly limbs, and their pointed teeth, but she hadn't. The creatures of the Deep still frightened her. Even as they helped her to exact her revenge.

"Don't give me that look," Irsa snapped, her eyes jerking from its fluttering fins.

"We are making the king look incompetent. Very soon his own people will turn against him in a bid to protect themselves."

"So you keep saying, but it's been nearly nineteen years, and I'm no closer to seeing this finished." Maybe she never would. Maybe she'd lose her memories before Tynan died. What then? Would what was left of her continue toward her goal even with her mind gone? Or would the creatures of the Deep just give up and go back to terrorizing easier prey?

"The king's daughter has been spotted outside of the walls," another voice wriggled into her mind, leaving the oily traces of an angler fish behind. Irsa suppressed a shudder.

"Which one?" the sea dragon asked, something like interest cutting through the monotone level of its thoughts.

"The youngest. Roan, I believe, is her name."

"We aren't hurting the children," Irsa said. She'd made up her mind about that long ago. She knew it'd be easier to hurt them. She knew they were Tynan's weak point, at least as far as his reputation was concerned. But they were also *hers*. Each one of the seven daughters had a piece of *her* in them, and Irsa couldn't bear to have more of *her* blood on her hands.

"The daughters are his weakness," the angler fish said, as if it had read her mind. It probably had. The communication was not one way between them, and Irsa did her best not to think about what that meant for her privacy. She knew full well that if the creatures of the Deep decided to turn on her, she'd given them enough ammunition long ago. No sense worrying about it now.

"We are not hurting the children," Irsa repeated, tone firm.

"Yes, Mistress," both creatures replied.

"But perhaps there is something that can be done with them that does not entail hurting them," the sea dragon pressed.

Irsa turned to look at it, narrowing her eyes on the smug satisfaction flowing out through its ungodly amount of orange fins. It had caught her interest, and it knew it. She jerked her head away to look back at the walled city.

"What did you have in mind?" she asked begrudgingly.

If a creature without shoulders could shrug, the sea dragon likely would have, but it couldn't, so it tilted its head to one side instead. "Everyone wants something. We are certain the young princess is no different. Why not meet with her and strike up a deal?"

"What would a princess want that she'd make a deal with the Witch of the Deep for? Especially when she has her own sea witch in the castle." Irsa's fingers were tapping on her bent tail again, pensive. She couldn't see why the youngest princess would have to want for anything. After all, Tynan no doubt spoiled her rotten.

"The same thing her mother wanted," the angler fish said. "Freedom."

Irsa laughed, soft and hollow, under her breath. Freedom. Of course, any child of *hers* would want that when all she had ever known was chains. They'd almost had it once, but it'd been snatched away.

"Gavril will not be keen to see to the princess Roan's whims. His master is Tynan, and no one else," the sea dragon added. "Only you could provide her with this."

"And what would I ask in trade? You know as well as I that a wish as large as that would come with a hefty price tag. What could the princess give me?"

The sea dragon just stared at her, unblinking. Irsa was tempted to say it was rolling its eyes at her. The angler fish swam from her side in a wide circle until it was right next to her ear.

"She could give you the king's pain. Think of what he would do if he lost his youngest and most precious daughter. The one who looked ever so much like his lost queen." The angler fish's voice was dark and slippery, its tone promising destruction and devastation. Painting a picture in Irsa's mind of a Tynan so ravaged by grief that he took his own life. That he allowed himself to slowly starve, perhaps. That he went mad, mad enough to finally drive his people to storm his castle walls and drag him to the surface for execution. It was a beautiful picture.

"All you need do is say the word, Mistress," the sea dragon cooed, "and we will find out the princess Roan's deepest wish so that you can grant it."

Something sick twisted in Irsa's belly. Guilt, probably. Trying to remind her that she'd always said she wouldn't touch *her* children. But it was different if she was granting Roan's wish, wasn't it? It would be different if she was giving the girl what she wanted. Surely *she* couldn't fault Irsa for that.

"You would be helping her," the angler fish insisted.

Irsa sighed and nodded. "Very well, gather what information you can, but do not engage. Not yet. Let's see what she wants before we make any promises."

"Yes, Mistress," both creatures agreed.

TWO

Roan

The walls of Alon were stifling, suffocating in a way Roan had only ever heard the air above the water could be. No one allowed out or in through the thick dome of magic engineered to keep the witch out, no one that was not escorted by at least half the royal guard. And the walls of the palace were even more heavily protected.

"Princess, shouldn't you be in lessons?" one of the soldiers posted at every single entrance and corridor asked. Siarl, she thought his name might have been, but there were so many of them these days it was harder and harder to keep track.

"Oh, no. I got out early," Roan said. Which wasn't technically a lie, as she *had* gotten out of lessons early. She just failed to mention that it was due to a minor sleeping spell on her tutor that had allowed her to *sneak* out. Tomorrow, when Chrysanta asked about it, Roan would say that she'd finished her studies while the older mer had been sleeping and left when she was done. Also not technically a lie; she had finished her studies.

"Ah, of course." Siarl smiled at her, offering a low bow. "Shall I escort you back to your rooms, Your Highness?"

"No, thank you. I know the way." Roan pasted on a timid smile and ducked her head, hoping it would be enough to make Siarl feel that his suggestion was improper. Maybe then he'd leave her alone and she could get to that break in the garden wall before anyone noticed she was missing. She still had at least a couple hours of lessons; if she swam fast enough, she could make it to the drift yard and back before supper.

"Really, I must insist, Your Highness. Your father would think me remiss if I didn't ensure your safety."

Safety! Roan wanted to laugh. What was there to fear inside the palace walls? What could harm her here with guards posted everywhere she looked, and a dome of magic closing them in? This wasn't safety. It was a cage. It was a prison. She wasn't being protected, she was being shackled, her fins cut so she couldn't swim.

Siarl made a move to offer her his arm, and Roan swam back a little, her long red hair floating into her face.

"That won't be necessary, Danil," another voice cut in, stilling the guard's movements. An all too familiar voice. Fars swam forward, placing herself between the guard, apparently named Danil, and Roan. Roan ducked herself behind her eldest sister's long white gown and offered Danil a sheepish smile. "My sister and I have a date for tea. I was just looking for her."

"Yes, Your Highness." Danil blushed, backing away from the two princesses to his post, which he likely wasn't supposed to be leaving even if it were to escort a princess to her rooms.

"Please excuse us." Fars' smile was a mask of diplomacy, kind but carefully calculated to make everyone around her feel as if she were in complete control of the situation.

Which she often was. As Father had fallen more and more into his fight with the Witch of the Deep, Fars had been left to tend to the affairs of state, to look after their people.

Danil nodded, his back straightening against the wall.

Fars looped her arm through Roan's and swam past the mer. They were halfway down the hall when she looked back and called, "And Danil?"

"Yes, Your Highness?"

"Keep up the good work." Fars shot him a wink that left the man blushing even more brightly, the color a strange contrast to his kelp-green hair. The two sisters didn't let their laughter out until they were two corridors down for fear of being overheard.

"'Keep up the good work,' she says," Roan mocked through her chortles.

"What?" Fars tilted her head, dark purple hair sweeping into her eyes as she looked down at her youngest sister. "Is there a problem with giving someone a compliment?"

"Oh no. Not at all. It's just, I never thought I'd see the day that Princess Fars would use blatant misdirection and manipulation and *flirting*." Roan shook her head, her chuckles slowly dying down. "Really, if Father knew . . . "

"Do you want me to help you to get out of the city or not?" Fars eyed her sister blandly. "Because if that wasn't a cry for help back there, I can just leave you to your own devices. I do have other duties to see to. I am in charge of the—"

"No! No. Please, Fars. Oh master of the tides of men's hearts—"

"And women's."

"And women's," Roan conceded with a nod. "Please help me escape the confines of my gilded prison so that I may swim freely in the open ocean, and—"

"All right. All right. All right." Fars rolled her eyes.

"Honestly, you're really pitiful sometimes, Roan. Why can't you be like our other sisters and just sit still and look pretty? It would make my life much easier."

"Because I'm not pretty." Roan huffed, rubbing the tip of her freckled nose with her finger.

Fars clicked her tongue but didn't say anything as they swam past another set of guards perched at the entrance to the royal gardens. The gardens were fairly empty this time of day. The servants and guards had their tasks, the king and his sea witch were both holed up in his office discussing this latest attack from the Witch of the Deep, and the king's daughters were all supposed to be in lessons or otherwise occupied. That left Fars and Roan free to swim leisurely deeper into the dense maze of seaweed and kelp until they reached the back wall.

"Pretty isn't everything you know," Roan said, throwing Fars' own words back to her and tugging on the satchel she'd tucked into the dense growth of coral along the wall.

"Yes, yes, I know, my little ugly guppy." Fars crooked her finger and tapped it on the tip of Roan's nose. "Just be back in time for supper, yes? I don't want to have to lie to Father about where you were again."

"I know. I know."

"And don't go to the surface. Let's not tempt fate a second time."

"Yes ma'am." Roan huffed, her breath making the red bangs hanging in her eyes float upward.

"And no—"

"No magic. Fars, I know! I'll be careful, I promise." Roan held up a hand, her fingers all pressed together as if she were swearing an oath. "I'll be good, and I'll make it back in time for supper."

"All right then. Have fun." Fars leaned in and pressed a

kiss to her sister's forehead, making Roan grumble. "Oh, stop that. Go on then, get out of here."

Roan didn't have to be told twice. She pushed her way through the little crack in the wall at the back of the garden and was out into the city before anyone noticed. From there, it was the work of ten minutes to sneak down the back streets of Alon to part of the wall that Fars had discovered was less patrolled than others. Roan paused for a moment to look around, then she swam up the length of the wall and over, through the wall of the domed barrier, with none being the wiser.

She was several feet out into the open ocean, the rocky outcroppings hiding her from the sight of the wall's guards, when she saw the little orange and yellow sea dragon. It flicked its fins in greeting, looking quite happy to see her.

"Oh? Were you waiting for me?" Roan offered the creature a wide smile and reached out to tap the top of its head, careful to avoid the leaf-like fins near the front.

The creature nodded.

"I hope you weren't waiting long. I got a little tied up with my sister," Roan said as she began to swim along the edge of the rocky crag.

The creature didn't say anything; it never did. Roan was used to having one sided conversations with the fish around her. The sea dragon who had taken to escorting her on her wanderings was no different.

"One of the guards caught me sneaking out of my lessons," she whispered conspiratorially. "Thankfully, my sister was there to help."

They swam further out, past the Jellyfish Forest and out to a big open space of ocean where the tide tended to drag all the best bits of debris from the surface. Great pieces of wood stuck out from the sand, their angles looking jagged and dangerous in the warm afternoon light as schools of fish darted between them.

"All right then." Roan braced her hands on her hips. "Let's get started."

She spent the next couple of hours with the little creature beside her, digging through the rubble left over from ships until her satchel was laden with trinkets.

The sea dragon nudged the overfull bag with its snout as if to ask, *What's all this stuff for?*

"Hm?" Roan's hands stilled where she'd been trying to pry a clay teapot from under a large bit of wood.

The creature nudged the bag open and swam inside before pushing out a comb of smooth, light-colored stone onto the sand.

"Oh. I just think it's neat." Roan shrugged before giving the deep red handle another hard yank. It came away more easily now that she'd worked it loose and sent her spiraling across the open water with a loud yelp. She pulled herself upright in the water, turning her latest treasure over and over in her hands with a little smile.

"The humans make such interesting things, don't you think? They're so . . . Hm . . . " She hummed, trying to think of the word, tapping her fingers against her freckled chin.

The sea dragon tilted its head in question.

"Innovative!" Roan snapped her fingers, looking up at the dark eyes of her friend with a wide smile. "They don't have magic, at least most of them don't, and yet look what they can make. Isn't it amazing?"

The sea dragon tilted its head the other direction. Roan was fairly sure that was a skeptical look.

"No, really! Look. Look at this." She swooped down to pick up the comb the sea dragon had been poking at. "We carve our combs from coral and old bones, but this is . . .

this is something else. It's some kind of stone. And it's all shiny, and pretty, and—"

A whale cried overhead, and Roan looked up to watch the small pod drift across the fading light from above.

"Oh, tides! It's getting late! I have to get back!" She quickly stuffed the teapot into her bag, as well as the comb, and started back the way she'd come. Bubbles streaked past her as her green tail flicked in the water. "If I'm late one more time, Fars will never cover for me again!"

The sea dragon struggled to keep up, using what magic its little body possessed to stay alongside the wayward princess as they raced back toward the city.

THREE

Irsa

———

"Humanity." The word wriggled through Irsa's mind, dragging her thoughts from the spell book she'd managed to scavenge from the rubble of a village.

"What?" she asked, black meeting black as she stared into the eyes of the little squid who had decided to come into her office without so much as an 'excuse me.'

"Humanity," it repeated, as if it were obvious. With squids, Irsa always felt like she was coming in halfway through a conversation. They'd pop up and say something completely innocuous and expect her to make the connection without any explanation. At least the others made sense, but not squids. Or jellyfish, come to think of it. She had once wondered why that was but had long since decided it didn't matter.

"All right. What about humanity?"

The squid's many tentacles flicked irritably, eyes narrowing into slits. Wonderful, now she'd offended it.

"You're going to have to be more specific." Irsa sighed, leaning back into the chair she'd perched on to wait patiently for the creature to gather its words. "What about humanity are we talking about here?"

"Roan," it supplied, as if that made everything make sense. It didn't. It was still squinting at her like she was a particularly stupid crustacean. Which was beyond rude.

"Roan?"

"Princess."

"Can I get more than one word at a time?"

The squid jerked, dispelling ink in a petulant huff.

"Well, that's not helping anyone, now is it?" Irsa crossed her arms over her chest. Either the creature would get to the point, or it would swim off somewhere. Irsa didn't care one way or the other so long as she got back to her work.

The squid squirted more ink at her.

"What it means to say," a sea dragon said as it glided through the water to hover just over her desk, long fins brushing the discarded book's pages. "Is that the princess Roan is interested in humanity. We would even wager that she perhaps would like to be human."

"What?" Irsa eyed the sea dragon narrowly, ignoring the squid as it sulked off to spill its ink elsewhere, hopefully away from her spell books.

"The princess Roan is interested in—"

"No. I heard you the first time. I'm just unclear on what this means for me, exactly." Irsa leaned forward to brace her elbows on the driftwood desk, pressing her face closer to the sea dragon's. "Is that her greatest wish?"

"It is."

"I can't turn her human. Find something else." Irsa turned back to her book, effectively dismissing the little creature. But she saw out of the corner of her eye that it didn't move.

"Cannot or will not?"

Irsa's fingers clenched where she held the book, wrinkling the pages at the edges. She paid it no mind, dropping it back to the desk with a decisive thud.

"What are you getting at, little monster?" she asked, her magic swelling within her to produce short tentacles of purple power in the water around her tail.

"You are powerful enough. We have given you all that you need to perform any spell you should so choose. Why is it that you cannot?" The sea dragon looked at her as if it was equal parts bored and unimpressed.

"I don't have a book with a spell for that in it. No one has ever performed that magic. If they have, they never wrote it down." Irsa foolishly hoped that would be enough to dissuade the creature. Or at least put it off for a while.

"You know very well that you do not need a book, or even spells, to perform magic. We have provided you with enough power to—"

"Yes, yes, I know, boil the sea if I so chose. I recall. But there are some things that are not done. Things that go against the grand design of Amiphrite herself. This is one of them."

"You performed unnatural magic for her mother once."

"And it nearly killed her!" Irsa spat. A sinking feeling settled into the pit of Irsa's stomach.

"But it did not. If we recall, the magic that killed her was Gavril's." The sea dragon was being far too reasonable, and Irsa had to wonder why. It couldn't just be to suit her purposes. There had to be more, but she didn't think she'd get a straight answer from it. "When you performed the magic, you were able to keep her alive."

"Only just," Irsa breathed, her eyes squeezing shut to try to will away the memory of *her* pale faced and weak. Why could the creatures of the Deep take her name but not that memory? Not the dreadful way her hands shook, or how close she had come to . . . Too close, and at Irsa's hands. "Plus, the human world, it's . . . it's dangerous. To send her up there would be sentencing her to death."

"You do not know that."

"I do!" Irsa's teeth ground together, frustration seething into her veins, hot and angry. "I do know that."

"You do not."

"Why are you pushing so hard for this?" Irsa asked, opening her eyes to squint at the creature suspiciously. "There has to be something else. Why this?"

"It is what the princess wants."

"Is it? Has she specifically said that she wishes she could be human?" Irsa tilted her head, watching the sea dragon shift its fins at her. It was being evasive, and she didn't like it.

"Not as such."

"Not as such?"

"Not as such."

"What does that mean? Either she has said those words or she hasn't."

"The princess has a great interest in human culture. She regularly collects items from the drift yard to keep as personal treasures." If Irsa didn't know any better, she'd say the creature sounded affronted, even as its tone remained completely even. "It is clear that she would enjoy being human, at least for a time, to study their culture up close."

"Well, that's not happening."

The sea dragon stared at her in thought, its head tilted to one side. "What if we were to tell you that her soulmate was human? Would you keep them separated? Would you subject the daughter of your soulmate to the same pain you and she faced?"

"Her soulmate is human?" Irsa frowned.

"Yes. Would you subject Roan to the same loneliness—"

"I heard you the first time!" Irsa growled, the book

snapping itself shut on her desk. She tossed it to the sand beside her where a stack of other tomes had taken up residence over the last few hours. "But it wouldn't be the same, would it? She and I . . . We were . . . We were together since birth. The princess and this human have never met. Neither will ever know what they're missing."

The sea dragon twitched as if to argue further about this matter but then seemed to think better of it and said simply, "Then perhaps we can provide her a window into the human world. A glimpse so that she can sate her curiosity. Perhaps that will be enough. It would be small magic, for you."

"That, I can provide." Irsa nodded, pushing off from her chair and swimming toward the door. "I just need a mirror, and for you to tell me when she'll be out at the drift yard next."

"Why?" The sea dragon swam along behind her.

"So I can give it to her, of course. You can't very well carry it, can you?"

"No, Mistress. We will let you know when her next visit to the drift yard is."

"Right then, off with you," Irsa said, not even turning to look at the creature as she swam toward the supply closet, already creating a mental list of what she'd need for such a spell.

"Yes, Mistress."

HER CHANCE CAME NOT but a handful of days later, when Irsa was sitting on one of her regular dunes examining the latest spells Gavril had woven into their shields to keep her out. They were nothing she couldn't break, if she wanted to. Gavril had never been terribly creative, and his defensive work was more blunt instrument than anything else. Still, it would be a bit of a nuisance.

"She is here, Mistress," a young voice rippled across her mind. The sea dragon was not close, but the creatures of the Deep seemed to be able to reach out across many leagues without expending much energy at all, so long as the link had already been established.

"I'll meet you at the drift yard." Irsa rose from her spot and started in that direction.

"Yes, Mistress."

The seal-lined bag Irsa used to collect ingredients tapped softly on her side as she made her way across the sand. Roan had a head start, but Irsa didn't want it to look like she was following her. She'd have to loop around and enter the drift yard from the other side.

Irsa paused about midway through the debris, tucking behind a bit of wood as the red-headed princess came into view. She wasn't sure what she'd thought it would be like to see the daughter of her love, especially the one who was heralded to look so much like her mother, but Irsa hadn't thought it would stop her heart the way it did. She found herself forgetting to breathe. The face wasn't the same, the nose a little longer, the lips a little thinner, but the hair was the same violent shade of red, and when the girl smiled and chatted with the sea dragon at her side, Irsa could see *her* in Roan.

"Mistress," the sea dragon murmured in her head, jolting her from her revery.

"Right," Irsa whispered, and straightened up from behind the jagged piece of ship. She swam out a little, putting herself perfectly into Roan's line of sight, and made herself look busy. Or as busy as one could look when they were swimming in the middle of a massive field of drift debris with their hands on their hips as if surveying the land.

"Oh! Hello!" Roan called, waving when Irsa turned to look at her.

Irsa waved back.

"I didn't think anyone else would be out here at this time of day." Roan laughed, making her way over to Irsa.

Irsa suppressed a frown. The princess hadn't even stopped to wonder if the mer she was approaching could be a danger to her or not. How naive was she? Her mother would never have — Irsa shook herself to dispel the thought.

"I'm not, usually," Irsa said, swallowing down a silent scream as the girl got closer and her features came more into focus. From further away, Irsa could see the similarities between Roan and her mother, but up close, only the differences were clear. Roan had her mother's red hair, but it was a shade darker, and everything else was Tynan's family. The angular jaw of the late queen. The straight nose of Roan's father. Even the tail color was just a shade off from how *hers* had been, a shade bluer. It was all . . . wrong. So wrong. Like looking at *her* through colored glass.

"I just needed to pick up a few things."

"Of course. Of course." Roan nodded, her smile spread wide over her face, making her eyes crinkle at the edges. Even those, Irsa was sure, were a shade or two off from Roan's mother's. "What were you looking for? Maybe I can help you. I'm out here all the time."

"You are?" Irsa asked, tilting her head. "Whatever for?"

"I just . . . I find it . . . interesting." Roan shrugged, looking sheepish. "So, what are you looking for?"

"I needed a couple items for a spell. A mirror. Some of the pottery. Any amulets if they're out here." Irsa hummed, thoughtfully, making a show of looking around herself and moving aside a piece of wood to check beneath it. This was all carefully rehearsed, practiced over and over a hundred times as she tried to get the wording right. She needed for Roan to wish for the thing so she could give it to her, but she'd have to lead Roan there first.

"What kind of spell?" Roan bent down to help Irsa look for the things she'd listed. "Hopefully it's not something bad."

"No, nothing like that. It's just a window spell." Irsa dug through the sand, finding a few bits of broken pottery to tuck into her bag.

"A window spell? I've never heard of that." Roan was watching her now, head tilted, eyes curious. "What does it do?"

"It lets me look out any window in the world." Irsa shrugged.

"*Any* window?"

"Mhm."

"Even maybe . . . a human window?"

Irsa straightened up, forcing her eyes wider. "Well, I suppose so. I've never thought to use it on a human window before."

"Oh, what I'd give to be able to look out a human window," Roan breathed. "To see what all goes on in their world."

"Did you have a particular window in mind?" Irsa pulled out the little hand mirror she'd tucked into her bag, tapping her fingers on it.

"No." Roan frowned, but she'd swum closer and was now peering over Irsa's shoulder. "Does this one have a window spell on it?"

"It does, but it shows Tjena. See?" The reflection shifted to show the view from a shop in Tjena. Irsa and Roan watched as mer swam down the street of one of the few villages Irsa hadn't attacked in years past, going about their business. "If you wanted, I could alter it for a human window."

"Really?!"

Irsa winced at the squeal but nodded just the same. That had been the plan. She'd even chosen a place already. A thriving shopping center where Roan would see plenty of the world on land.

"Please. I'll give anything. Please." Roan swam around Irsa to float in front of her, her hands clasped to her chest, begging. "Please."

"Help me find the things I need to make another, and I'll happily alter this one for you."

Roan nodded quickly and spun around to begin her search. A couple of hours later, Irsa's bag was weighed down with bits of pottery, amulets, and mostly unbroken mirrors. She altered the spell on the little hand mirror and handed it over to Roan, who watched with rapt attention as a woman in a broad-brimmed hat with a long feather tucked into the band strutted past.

"This . . . this is magnificent," Roan said, her hands clutching the mirror. Then she swam forward and hugged Irsa long and hard. "This means so much to me. Great Poseidon, thank you! This is wonderful."

"No need." Irsa pulled the girl's arms from around her awkwardly and put some space between them. "Just be sure to enjoy this gift from . . . " She paused, about to say her name, and then thought better of it. "Your auntie."

"Yes, Auntie!" Roan laughed, glee lining her features, and for a moment, just a brief moment, Irsa saw *her* there. *Her* face lit up as she twirled in a dark green dress that matched her tail. Happiness making her eyes crinkle.

A whale cried overhead, and Roan jerked her head upward to look at the humpbacks that swam between them and the light from above.

"Oh, that's my sign to go home. Thanks again for this, Auntie! I'll never forget you!" Roan called over her shoulder, already halfway to the edge of the drift yard.

Irsa waved her goodbyes, and once she was sure Roan wasn't looking anymore, dumped all the junk out of her satchel and turned to head home.

FOUR

Roan

It was magnificent, being able to sit and just watch the humans walk about, doing whatever it was they did all day. Every one of them seemed to be going someplace, and in such a hurry too. Roan supposed that made sense, as human lives were so very short when compared to a mer, who could live forever given the right circumstances.

Roan had been watching them for a fortnight, and she still hadn't grown tired of them. Thoughts of the human world had taken up residence in her mind every day and night, making it difficult to concentrate on anything else. She could only hope her tutors hadn't noticed. Or if they had, they'd keep their suspicions to themselves.

"And so, in short, that is how your great grandfather, the king Beynon, defeated the great kraken," Chrysanta droned, her tone flat enough to make even the most rousing of adventure stories sound boring.

Great Grandfather had fought a kraken for Poseidon's sake, that should have been exciting! And yet, all Roan could think about was the sweet little baker boy who had given an extra roll to the little girl from the hat shop, and how she'd turned as red as a sea anemone over it. It had been terribly adorable.

"Are you listening, Your Highness?" Chrysanta asked, her tone sharp as she perched her hands on her hips.

"Yes, Chrysanta." Roan nodded quickly, sitting up straighter in her chair. "I was wondering though . . . Do you think the humans know that Great Grandfather saved them from the kraken?"

"What?" Chrysanta's eyes were wider, near bulging from her skull, and Roan thought maybe she should quickly backtrack, but she was curious.

"Well, it's just, as you said, the kraken was causing devastating tsunamis. I'm sure they were destroying the humans' homes and their livelihoods."

"King Beynon did not save humans." Chrysanta sniffed, affronted.

"But he did. The kraken would have destroyed anything along the coast, maybe even beyond, if it were left to its own devices. It didn't care about those people, it cared about destruction and feeding. It would have gotten bigger and bigger. Who's to say what would have happened had Great Grandfather not stepped in." It made sense to Roan. Maybe those humans did appreciate her great grandfather's interference. Maybe they held a festival in his honor. She would never know, but she wanted to. And she had to wonder if someone did know. If somewhere, some scholar had taken note of human history.

"That is not the point of this lesson, young miss. We do not interfere in the humans' affairs, and you know that well enough. Nor do we make ourselves known to them. If he did save those humans, they would never have known about it." Chrysanta's eyes had narrowed on her young

charge, and Roan shifted in her seat. "Now, as I was saying
. . . "

The lesson dragged on, and Roan's mind wandered
back to the cute little baker boy and the girl from the hat
shop. She was sure they didn't have to sit through boring
history lessons.

ROAN HAD BEEN DIGGING in the library for hours. She'd
found books on virtually everything except the thing she
wanted to read about. There was a book on common fishing
routes the humans took so that the mer could avoid them at
all costs. A book on human weapons and fishing supplies so
that the mer could combat them. And even a map of the
land formations and how they seemed to be divided up by
region. That was actually sort of interesting, and Roan had
spent a fair number of minutes studying it.

But there were no books on human history. No books
on what they wore, how they spoke, their advancements as
a society. Nothing to teach her about their world outside of
the dangers they posed to her people.

Roan nudged one of the books aside so she could sprawl
onto her back on the kelp rug and pull the mirror from her
bag. The weather was turning there, growing warmer, and
the humans had begun to carry around these strange things
with a long handle and a domed barrier to block out the
sun. They were really quite pretty, with plenty of frills and
lace. Roan just couldn't understand why they'd want to
block out the sun . . . She shook her head.

"I'm telling you, Your Highness, there is something off
about her as of late," a hushed voice carried through the
shelves to where Roan had tucked herself into the back of
the library. "She's been asking strange questions in class,

and I heard from one of the palace scribes that she's been digging around in the library looking for books on humans."

"It's just idle curiosity, Gavril. Nothing to worry about," Father said. "Aislin was the same way. Always digging into things she found interesting for a while and then flitting off to the next thing. It'll pass."

Roan turned onto her stomach, dropping the mirror beside her bag so she could swim close to the floor over to a shelf. Peeking through a space between books, she saw Father and his sea witch on the other side of the library. Gavril looked furious, but Father didn't seem upset at all. He didn't care what Roan did so long as she stayed out from under fin and didn't get herself hurt before she was old enough to marry. He'd always made that abundantly clear to her. Her only requirement was to make a good match.

"No one wants a curious wife," Gavril huffed.

Father shrugged. "She'll grow out of it. She'll accept her duty, just as her mother did. Honestly, Gavril, we have far more pressing matters."

"She's been off to the drift yard. As recently as last week." Gavril's voice echoed through the water, floating around the current as it drifted to Roan, even for how low his tone was. "She has a whole collection of human *things* in her rooms."

Roan stilled, her breath catching in her throat. How did he know? How had Gavril found out?

Father's back stiffened, and he turned slowly to look at Gavril, fury tracing every line of his back. "What?!"

"Oh tides," Roan squeaked, and turned to gather up her things. She needed . . . she needed to . . . she needed to hide . . . *everything*.

"You asked me to keep an eye on them, all seven of them, and I have." Gavril's tone had turned smug. "Your youngest is entirely too clever and curious for her own good. At first I thought it was just—"

"I want her rooms searched. Now!" Father spun, swimming toward the one door of the library. Gavril followed behind, his tail twitching with poorly hidden pleasure.

Roan gathered up her things, stuffing them back into her bag, and swam after them. All she could hope was that she'd make it back to her rooms before Father could. She turned the opposite direction and raced through the corridors of the palace, ignoring guards and servants as she made her way to her room. When she got there, Father and Gavril hadn't arrived yet. So she threw her bag onto the bed and began tucking away some of the more incriminating items.

She was just pushing a basket of small wooden sticks and shiny cutlery under her bed when the door burst open.

"Father!" Roan squeaked. "What . . . uh . . . What brings you here?"

She nudged the basket further under the bed with the tip of her fin, hoping the woven seagrass blanket would hide it.

"You have been out to the drift yard." Father motioned for four mer to follow him into her room and begin their search.

"I have not," she lied.

Apparently not well. Father eyed her blandly.

"I have not," she said, trying to sound stronger.

"What have I told you about leaving the palace? What have I told you about leaving Alon?"

"It's dangerous." Roan's shoulders sagged with guilt. "Something could happen to me."

"Exactly. And yet you defy me!"

"Father, I didn—"

But the lie was lost when one of the mer turned out the

bottom drawer of her dresser to reveal the pottery she'd carefully tucked amongst her spare blankets.

"And then you have the audacity to lie!" Father swam closer, grabbing her by the shoulders giving her a hard shake that made her head bobble. "To my face!"

"Should we continue, Your Highness?" one of the mer asked, looking between Father and Roan uncomfortably.

"Yes. All of it. Search all of it. And whatever you find, I want destroyed. Take it out to the practice fields and have it blasted to bits." Father's voice had gone cold, his fingers pressed hard enough into Roan's shoulders to leave prints behind.

"Father, no. These are just . . . they're just things. They aren't hurting anyone. I'm not hurting anyone by keeping them." Roan met his eyes, hoping to sway him, as she swallowed down the tears. "I promise I won't go out anymore, but please leave me what I have?"

And then Father did something he'd never done in all of Roan's life. He drew back his hand and smacked Roan across the cheek hard enough to make her teeth rattle against each other. She tasted blood on her tongue, and she tried to struggle away from him, to shrink back from any further blows. But there was nowhere to go, and his grip was unyielding.

The men dragged more and more of Roan's little treasures out, dumping them onto the rug in the middle of her room. Bits of jewelry and crockery. Old mirrors and pictures half destroyed by water. Enough evidence to expose her lies to Father and then some.

Roan watched it all as it was dumped into a pile carelessly.

"I will break you of this infernal curiosity yet," he hissed, grabbing her jaw roughly and forcing her to look at him.

"You won't." It was hard to talk around the hold he had on her face, but Roan would not be cowed. Not by Father, not by anyone.

"What was that?"

Roan jerked her face out of his grip, refusing to lift a hand to rub at her already bruising skin. "I said, you will not. You will not break me. Just as you did not break my mother."

Roan saw the next smack coming, but that didn't mean she could avoid it. She took the blow with clenched teeth and narrowed eyes.

"We will see about that." Father released her, pushing her back toward the bed where she sprawled across the blankets. "Take it away. All of it. And see that you post two guards outside of the princess' door at all hours. She is to go nowhere unescorted."

"Yes, Your Highness." The mer bowed and began to collect all of Roan's treasures. When they left, Father ahead of them, they left nothing behind, not even a broken bit of pottery.

The door slammed behind them, and Roan sat there for a moment, looking around at her rooms that felt suddenly empty without her treasures. For but a moment, Roan almost let the tears take over. They burned and itched at her eyes, begging to be shed. But then she sucked in a breath and pulled herself up. Tears wouldn't do her any good, not now.

Still, she thought, flopping onto her back in the middle of her bed, it wasn't like there was anything that could be done. She could run away, yes. Escape into the sea. But Father and his soldiers would find her. She couldn't get far enough fast enough to outpace them, she was sure of that. And she didn't know enough magic to disguise herself in the meantime either.

She huffed, rolling onto her side, and something glinted from the depths of her bag. Reaching over, Roan pulled the mirror out.

"Auntie knows plenty of magic." Roan smiled, a plan already forming in her mind.

FIVE

Irsa

"She is coming. She is coming. She is coming." The words slithered and writhed and wriggled through the current and into Irsa's mind. They were thought in all different tones and volumes and octaves, as if a hundred dark creatures were crying out.

Irsa squeezed her eyes shut, trying to blot them out. Now wasn't the time to get wrapped up in their excitement; she had other matters to deal with. Like the new wards Gavril had put up that kept her from seeing into the palace. She needed eyes in there to know if Tynan planned to strike back at her. She was not taking any chances in this war.

"Mistress," a voice called, this one far closer and louder than the others.

Irsa yelped, her eyes flying open as her hand moved to clutch at her chest.

"What have I told you about sneaking up on me?" She shook a finger at the sea dragon.

"Apologies, Mistress." It bowed its head to her, taking on the facade of remorse, but Irsa knew better. She knew it got some sort of twisted amusement from startling her. "Have you heard the news, Mistress?"

"What news?" Irsa ducked her head back to the text she'd been pouring over, scratching notes into the bit of parchment beside it on her desk.

"She is coming."

"Oh yes, I heard that. The depths seem to be in quite the uproar over it." Irsa shrugged, not taking her eyes off her work. Either the creature would get to a point, or it would leave. She didn't have time to play mind games with it, and it had to know that.

"The princess will need a caretaker when she is on land. A human to protect her, and show her how things are done." The sea dragon spoke as if picking up a thread of conversation that they'd both already been participating in. "We might suggest her soulmate, as he is the most likely to care about her."

"Fine. Fine." Irsa waved the creature off, her mind already deep within the text in front of her again. There had to be a way around Gavril's annoying thick wall of . . . Wait. "What? The princess needs a what?"

"A caretaker. She needs someone to look after her in the human world to see that she does not get into trouble."

Irsa's eyes narrowed on the creature, a frown tugging at her lips. "She's going to ask me to give her legs."

"In all fairness, Mistress, you gave her the idea." The sea dragon sounded smug. "You gave her the mirror so that she could see the human world for herself. It is not her fault that it did not sate her curiosity."

"You tricked me," Irsa hissed. "You knew this would happen."

"We did not. We had no way of knowing that the king would find out about her collection of human items and create a rift between himself and his daughter. We had no way of knowing that she would determine this was her only method of escape." The creature bobbed in the water carelessly.

"What did Tynan do to her?" The words scraped Irsa's throat raw. Her mind raced to all of the things he could have done to drive a wedge between himself and Roan. Tynan had never been a particularly violent man, at least not when Irsa had known him, but he had been cold and calculating. He could be cruel when fury struck him, and he saw the mer in his life as one might a seahorse: not as people at all but property. Irsa was sure Roan was no different.

"We do not know the particulars. All we know is that the guards were seen destroying her collection of human items on the training fields this morning, and someone has been siphoning off magic since."

"Siphoning off magic?"

"We believe the princess intends to escape. She will need magic to do so if she is to get past the guards and Gavril's new wards."

Irsa nodded, tapping her fingers on the parchment beneath her palm. She had no idea how strong Roan was, but at her age, to gather enough magic to escape without being noticed would take time. A day or two at the very least.

"How long do you think I have?"

"We estimate that it will take the princess at least four days to escape, even with her elder sister's help."

"Good. That gives me a little time to track down her soulmate and convince him to look after her on land." Irsa rose from her chair to move to the shelves along the wall. She'd need to locate the man first, and then she'd have to somehow get him to meet with Roan and stay with her. It shouldn't be too hard once she found him; soulmates were naturally drawn to one another.

"You are aware that if you do this, the king will think you took his daughter."

Irsa stilled, her fingers grasping the spine of a book. She bit her lip and nodded slowly. "I am aware."

"It will mean war."

"It will. Are you and the others going to back out now that we're so close?"

"No, Mistress. We just needed you to know what this means."

Irsa took a deep breath and pulled the book from the shelf. There was no going back now. This war with Tynan had already cost her too much. She couldn't stop when she was so close. She began examining the other texts, and the sea dragon was silent behind her for several long moments.

When its thoughts pressed into Irsa's mind again, it sounded almost sad. "This will cost that girl quite a bit."

"It doesn't have to." Irsa piled another book on top of the stack in her arms.

"Mistress?"

"Go and inform the others," Irsa said, not answering the creature's question.

"Yes, Mistress."

FINDING THE MAN, as it turned out, was the easy part. Irsa had gotten lucky in that he was currently staying in a port town of one of the larger continents. She wasn't sure what she'd have done if he were somewhere inland, but she supposed she'd have made do.

"To give yourself legs for a day will —"

"Yes, yes, cost me two days' worth of memories. I know

the trade, sea dragon." Irsa rolled her eyes, her fingers working the intricate patterns of the spell as magic hummed around them.

They'd found a cave along the shore connected to the sea by a deep tunnel which stretched beneath the sands. Irsa could see the gloomy rocks just above the surface. It wasn't ideal, but she couldn't exactly crawl along the beach with a tail and hope Fumihiro Jiro found her and not someone else. Then there would be the matter of explaining the tail or bewitching him into not noticing it. If she had to use magic to convince him to help her . . . Well, she didn't think two mind-altering spells were a good thing for the human brain. She might addle the poor man, and then where would she be?

"Mistress, we are not sure that—"

"Oh? Now you're having second thoughts?" Irsa snapped.

"No, Mistress." The creature sighed, sounding thoroughly cowed.

"Good, because I don't have time for distraction. I'm a little busy here." Irsa kept her eyes firmly on the intricate weaving of the magic in her hands.

The image of a red-haired mer smiling up at her from where they sat in a room full of books was pulled to the forefront of Irsa's consciousness like a thread. They were in her office in the castle, her mind supplied. The mer was playing with Irsa's fingers, running her thumbs along the creases in her palm and humming a soft tune.

It took another few minutes before Irsa felt the magic settle over her fin like a net, then the memory was gone, unraveling like a worn blanket. The spell tightened, cutting off the circulation, and she winced. Irsa's hands fisted at her sides, squeezing her eyes shut as the magic began to cut into her scales, slicing her fin in two, leaving a trail of blood in the water that would no doubt draw sharks if any were near, and whittling the pieces away into legs.

"Tides!" Irsa choked through the pain of it. And then, all at once, it was over, leaving Irsa gasping for breath, inhaling water and choking on it when it filled her human lungs. She coughed, but that brought in more water.

"Mistress. The surface," the creature reminded her gently and pushed Irsa up to the surface where she was finally able to vomit out the water that had threatened to suffocate her weak human lungs.

"Honestly, how do they live like this?" she asked when she'd caught her breath.

"That is a discussion for another time, Mistress. Roan's soulmate will have heeded your call and be on the beach. You must meet him."

Irsa nodded and pulled herself up onto the sand, her legs kicking in the water below to try to propel her upward. But human feet made a spectacularly bad replacement for flippers.

"Strange," Irsa said, her fingers digging into the gritty surface below her palms as she pushed herself to stand.

"Mistress?"

"Sand is so much softer when it's under water." She picked up a handful of the stuff and let the texture scrape at her skin thoughtfully. Strange indeed.

Shaking herself, Irsa pressed her hands over her gauzy sea-silk dress. If she were going up into the human settlement, she'd need to change it. But she didn't think that was necessary now. Fumihiro Jiro would come to her.

And indeed, there was a dark-haired man standing out under the moon, watching the waves roll in, when Irsa exited the cave. He'd pushed a pair of spectacles off his nose and up into his hair to keep the long strands out of his eyes. It wasn't working; a few slipped free to sway in the breeze.

"Fumihiro Jiro?" Irsa asked, her bare feet leaving prints behind her in the sand as she made her way over to him.

His head snapped in her direction, dark eyes wide. "Are you . . . Are you . . . ?" His mouth gaped open and shut for a long moment, struggling for the words. "Are you a spirit?"

"I suppose I'm something like that." Irsa tilted her head, a wry smile tugging at her lips. A spirit.

"Right. Of course. Something like that." Fumihiro Jiro nodded, his gaze flicking back out to the water before they returned to her. "You called me out here."

"Yes, I did."

"What do you want with me?" He sounded afraid, but he wasn't backing away. He'd dug his heels into the sand and tilted his chin up in determination.

"I need you to do me a favor." Irsa wondered if this were the type of thing human spirits would do. Would they appear to humans and ask favors of them? She'd never heard of Poseidon or Amiphrite getting involved in their people's lives in such a way. But then, the mer had magic, and perhaps that was the difference.

"What sort of favor?" He narrowed his eyes.

"In two days' time, a girl will appear on the beach." He titled his head in question, and Irsa shook hers, laughing softly. "Not me, another girl. She will have red hair and freckles and brilliant green eyes. You are to help this girl. Look after her while she is here, in your world."

"What's her name?"

"Roan." Irsa smiled gently.

Fumihiro Jiro nodded. "Is that all?"

"That is all. Will you do me this favor?"

"Yes." He bowed his head to her, a show of respect for what this human considered to be a spirit. Irsa supposed, in the vague sense of things, perhaps she was a spirit. She had magic, unlike most humans, and she came from the water. Maybe that did make her a spirit to them after all.

"Do you not have a request in return?"

"No." Fumihiro Jiro shook his head, drawing more stray locks from beneath his spectacles. "I'll happily do this favor for you, spirit."

Irsa blinked for a moment. "Are you sure you don't have anything you'd like to ask for?"

"No. Thank you." He bowed his head again, keeping it bowed so long that his spectacles began to slip from their position.

"Very well. Thank you." Irsa nodded, and before she could think better of it, added, "And should you need anything, anything at all, come to the sea and call for Irsa. I'll be here."

"Thank you, Irsa."

SIX

Roan

$\mathcal{R}$oan peeked around the corner, holding her breath and praying to Poseidon that the guards down the corridor wouldn't look her way at exactly the wrong time.

Two. Four. Eight! Eight guards in the hallway leading to the gardens. Tides, that was a lot.

"You can't put them all to sleep," a voice said from right behind her.

Roan jerked, her hands flying to her mouth just in time to muffle her yelp as she spun to glare at her sister. Fars tilted her head, looking thoroughly amused at the glare her youngest sister shot her.

"Or were you *not* planning to sleep spell all of them and hope that no one noticed?" Fars asked, raising one purple brow.

"He hasn't exactly left me much choice." Roan dropped her hands from her lips, trying not to look petulant but failing miserably. "It's this or I just . . . stay here until he can find me a suitable husband."

"No, I suppose he hasn't." Fars sighed, swimming to the

corner so she could peek around it along with Roan. They backed away again, and Fars leveled a frown at Roan. "So, what is your plan then? If you manage to get out?"

"I was going to see that sea witch I met at the drift yard a couple of weeks ago. I thought maybe she could help me hide myself until I could get far enough away that they wouldn't find me." Roan adjusted the satchel on her shoulder. She'd only packed a spare tunic, the mirror, a dagger, and a journal, nothing else. Food she could find out in the open ocean. And she doubted she'd need any of her finery once she left the palace.

"Even with her help, they'll find you." Fars bit at her bottom lip thoughtfully. "It doesn't matter where you go."

"Maybe."

"No. He will." Fars shook her head. "That's why Mother never left."

"What?"

"Nothing. Look, he'll find you. So long as you're under the sea, you're in danger. And I don't know what Father will do with you when he does. I don't think he'd hurt you, but . . . " Fars' shoulders sagged. "I can guarantee you'd never be happy again."

"Then what do you suggest, Fars? I can't just . . . I can't stay here," Roan hissed, her eyes burning with unshed tears again. "I can't stay here and wait for him to marry me off to someone horrible. I can't . . . I can't . . . "

"You can't fade away like Mother did, I know." Fars swam forward, her hands taking hold of Roan's shoulders to give them a gentle squeeze.

Roan nodded weakly, inhaling a lung full of water and letting it calm her ragged heartbeat.

Fars watched her, her eyes narrowed in thought for a moment. Then she seemed to decide something. She nodded to herself and released Roan's shoulders before moving to swim past her in the opposite direction Roan had been headed.

"Follow me."

Roan opened her mouth to argue. To ask Fars what in the name of Poseidon she was thinking of. But Fars didn't wait for her to speak; she grabbed her sister's wrist and yanked her back the way she'd come.

They were halfway down a corridor that hadn't been used for as long as Roan had been alive when Fars finally slowed her pace. There were no guards in this wing of the palace, probably because of the eerie smells of still water and dark magic.

"Fars, where are we going?" Roan whispered, half afraid that if she were too loud, whatever was tainting the water around them would come after her next.

"This was Mother's wing." Fars' voice carried oddly through the still water. She lifted her hand to conjure a bit of witch light into her palm, its soft purple orb casting just enough light for them to swim by, and pressed on. "This is where she lived before she died."

"Why is it so . . . " Roan gestured around them as they swam deeper.

"This is also where the Witch of the Deep's office was when she lived here at the palace. Her books did this. Father tried to have them removed, but they just kept coming back. Like this was home." Fars squinted through the dark, looking for something. "The best Gavril could do was to seal off the corridor to keep the magic contained."

"*Books* did this?" Roan frowned.

"They had an interesting reaction when Mother passed. Ah. Here we are." Fars dropped Roan's wrist so she could push a door inward. On the other side was a large room with floor-to-ceiling shelves lined with almost as many books as the library held. In the center was a large driftwood desk, and off to one side sat a worn chaise.

"What is this place?" Roan swam deeper in, doing her best to ignore how the chill in the water made bumps rise on her arms.

"This was her office before Father expelled her from the palace."

"Why are we here?"

"Because this is the easiest way to get out of the palace without anyone noticing you. All the men are too afraid to come within ten feet of this place, even on the outside." Fars swam to the large window in between two of the towering bookshelves, dropping the witch light in the water to float beside her. "Help me."

Roan swam over, and between the two sisters, they managed to pry the window open.

"They don't patrol outside this window. Or anywhere near it. You should have a straight unhindered shot to the back wall and then out into the city." Fars reached up to unclasp the small shell she wore around her neck. "You'll need this though. Gavril has changed the wards to not allow anyone without a talisman in or out. You'll have to take mine."

"Father will know." Roan clutched the shell hard enough that she could feel its edges digging into her palm. "Fars, you'll get into trouble."

"I'd like to see him try to punish me." Fars scoffed. "Then who will take care of all the paperwork he keeps ignoring while he wages war against the Witch of the Deep?"

"Fars."

"Honestly, if he did, I'd be grateful. Then at least I'd get a break from performing all his duties while he —" Fars cut herself off, taking a deep breath and running a hand through her long violet hair. "Doesn't matter. The point is no one will see you. Just give me ten minutes to draw their attention to the south side of the gardens, and you'll be in the clear. All right?"

"All right." Roan nodded.

"And once you get to that witch," Fars started, her lips pressing together for a moment as if she didn't really want to say the next bit, but she knew she had to. "Once you get to her, you ask her to give you legs. At least for a little while. I know it'll make you happy, and you'll be safe on land. Maybe by the time you're done adventuring, this mess with Father and the Witch of the Deep will be cleared up."

"Fars . . . I don't know."

"Well, I do. You ask that witch to give you legs, and you go off and have yourself the adventure the rest of us can't have. The adventure Mother couldn't have. Are we clear?"

Roan nodded quickly, clutching the shell to her chest.

"Good." Fars leaned in to press a kiss to her sister's forehead. "Be safe, little sister. And be sure to keep a careful mental log of everything. I want lots of stories when you get back, all right?"

"All right."

Fars looked her over once more, then nodded to herself and swam out of the room. Roan waited ten minutes, and when she slipped through the window, just as Fars had said, no one noticed her.

THE SWIM to the drift yard took half the time it normally would have, or at least it felt that way with Roan's heart pounding in her chest. She heard nothing over the rush of water and her own fear.

She turned to look only once at the walls that lined

Alon, their rocks laced in magic from Gavril, just to see if anyone was following her. No one was. The water around the city rippled with its wards, but otherwise there was no movement. Not a single creature went in or out.

Nodding to herself, Roan spun and continued on. She had no idea where the witch lived, but she thought perhaps the drift yard was a reasonable start. Maybe the sea dragon who regularly waited for her could help. It was growing darker. Her family would be having supper soon. She wondered how Fars would cover for her. Maybe she'd say that Roan wasn't feeling well, or maybe she'd say that Roan was throwing a tantrum. Both were true, in their way.

The drift yard was empty when she finally reached it. The fading light from above reflected off bits and pieces of the lives of humans on the surface, but there was no movement. Not a single minnow darted between the jagged pieces of wood.

"Well, what were you expecting, Roan? That they'd just be sitting around waiting for you to show up?" Roan muttered to herself, dropping down to sit on a railing that protruded from the sand.

Alon glowed in the distance, the wards shimmering in the fading light like a dome protecting the city. They'd notice soon. If not tonight, then by morning. Father would send out a search party, and they'd be on her trail before she'd even gotten a league away. They'd drag her back, and she'd be forced to surrender to her fate.

Roan hunched, bracing her elbows on her bent tail. All of this would be for not.

"It's quite late to be scavenging for treasure, isn't it?" a voice called from behind her, and Roan spun, losing her balance and toppling from the narrow rail in her hurry. "Careful, don't hurt yourself."

Roan straightened her spine, running her hands over her dress to smooth it. "Auntie."

"What are you doing out here so late? Shouldn't you be home, safe in your bed?" The witch tilted her head, a fringe of white hair falling into her face.

"I ran away."

"You ran away?" The witch's white brows rose, half hidden by the fringe. "Whatever for?"

"I was . . . I couldn't . . . " Roan pressed her lips together, taking a breath.

The witch watched her struggle for a moment, then she shook her head and tsked softly. "Let's have this conversation elsewhere. They'll be looking for you soon, I'm sure."

Roan nodded and let the woman lead her away from the drift yard, toward the Jellyfish Forest, and into its depths where a small house stood. Once there, the witch pulled Roan down into a rotting plush chair and set about making them tea. Faint purple magic rippled around the woman as she heated the pot of water. By the time she pressed a small, chipped cup into Roan's hands, Roan felt her heartbeat had slowed.

"Thank you."

The witch said nothing, just settled into her own seat across from Roan and sipped from her cup. They didn't match. Roan wondered if she'd found them in the yard or if they were simply the remains of two different sets. The witch watched her, seemingly willing to wait till Roan was ready to speak.

After a couple of fortifying sips from her cup, Roan took a deep breath and lowered it to its saucer. "I came here to ask for you to give me legs."

"You want to be human?"

"Yes." Roan watched the witch's eyes narrow in thought, and she gripped her teacup more tightly where it rested warm against her scales. "Not for forever. Just for a time. A year, perhaps."

"Magic like that has a price. You understand that, don't you?"

"I do. I'm willing to pay it."

"I haven't even told you what the price will be yet." The witch frowned, setting aside her teacup to rise from her seat and move to a shelf stuffed full of books along the back wall of the small sitting room. Her fingers traced over their spines reverently. "What if it's something you're not willing to barter with?"

Roan swallowed, squeezing her eyes shut for a moment. What wouldn't she give for this chance? What could the witch ask for that Roan wouldn't lose if she didn't do this anyway? Nothing. The answer was nothing.

"I am willing to pay it."

The witch's shoulders hunched forward, but she didn't argue. She just grabbed a volume from the shelf and a small glass jar from her desk, then returned to her seat. Roan waited, her fingers tapping against the ceramic with soft *tinking* sounds.

"Your voice," the witch said after a silence that left Roan squirming.

"My voice?"

"Yes, that's what it will cost you. Your voice. I may be able to return it to you in a year's time when you give up your legs. But I cannot promise anything. If you need time to think about it, I can —"

"No! No. My voice." Roan nodded quickly enough to pull a few strands from the long braid down her back. They fluttered in the water around her. "I'll give you my voice."

The witch squinted at her, her black eyes flicking over Roan, and then nodded. "Follow me."

Roan set aside her tea and followed the witch through

her small home, out a back door, and into the depths of the Jellyfish Forest. By the time they emerged, the sea had grown black with night, only the witch's magic lit the way as they swam. Roan didn't ask where they were going, she supposed it didn't much matter at this point. She'd struck the deal, and soon she'd have her legs.

SEVEN

Roan

The witch led her to a small cave and then upward until they both surfaced. Roan's head flicked around, eyes trying to adjust to the darkness around her where the glow from the witch's magic could no longer reach.

"There is a beach just outside this cave," the witch said, pointing toward the opening, which was lit by a full moon in the distance. "I have lured a human here; he will ensure your safety once you're on land. Do you have any questions?"

Roan shook her head, her hair sticking to her face.

"Then let's begin." The witch ducked back under the surface, setting the witch light to float beside her, and then her hands began to work in slow, intricate patterns, echoing with the hum of magic from the witch's lips.

Roan watched wide eyed as the purple magic from before shimmered like scales around the witch's move-ments. It was beautiful. Roan had never seen magic worked like this before. Gavril always used compulsion to force the world around him to do his bidding. To break it down so that he could do with it what he chose. But this wasn't like Gavril's magic, all angry and hard. This was softer, like the witch was praying to the magic, asking it to fulfill her wishes, and it was answering those requests by bending to her will.

"One day, you'll have to teach me to do that," Roan whispered reverently.

The witch looked up from her hands, her face twisting into something complicated that Roan couldn't explain. Longing, perhaps. Then it was gone, and her black eyes flicked back down to her hands. "Maybe one day I will."

Roan opened her mouth to thank her, but the witch shook her head, stopping the words on her tongue.

"I need you to sing."

"I don't . . . All right." Roan nodded and took a breath before beginning the soft lullaby that Fars had sung to her since she was a babe. It was a simple song, and she'd forgotten half the words long ago, but she didn't think it would matter.

For a moment, nothing happened. The witch worked the spell with her hands, and Roan sang. But then Roan felt the song start to crawl up her throat. Not as it would if she were singing it but as if it were a living thing and it had decided it needed to get out. She choked on the feeling, coughing, but it kept moving. Up, and up, and up, until it sat behind her teeth. She tried to swallow around it, but it wouldn't budge. Then it forced itself past her lips. It floated, a little bundle of rippling water, into the jar that the witch had brought with her. She sealed it with a cork.

"This next part is going to hurt," the witch warned, and then her hands began to move in shorter, sharper patterns. The magic flared dark and dangerous, glowing still but with a deeper light. It left the witch's hands and wrapped around

Roan's tail, tight, tighter, cutting off the circulation to her fins and the very tip of her tail.

Then it was cutting into her scales, scraping them away. Carving down the center of her tail to separate it into two. Roan was glad her voice was gone; she didn't want to hear the silent scream that was ripped from her throat, leaving it raw. She didn't want to know what kind of sounds a mer could make when they were in that much pain. She squeezed her eyes shut against the black spots that swam across her vision. Her breath came in ragged, hard pants.

And then, all at once, the pain was gone, and she was choking on the water around her. It filled her lungs as it always had, but her body reacted differently to it.

This must be what drowning feels like, she thought.

The witch grabbed her around the waist and propelled them to the surface. When they pushed through the water, into the cave, Roan grasped at the sand beside the deep pool, coughing. The witch patted her back hard, helping to get the water from her lungs. Once she had, Roan took a deep, grateful breath, letting it fill her up as her feet flicked uselessly in the water.

She wasn't sure how long she hung there on the edge of the pool, just breathing as the witch rubbed soothing circles into her back. The witch pushed her up onto the sand entirely, lifting her wrinkled feet out of the water.

"Go out that opening and head toward the east. There will be a man waiting for you. His name is Fumihiro Jiro, and he'll look after you."

Roan opened her mouth to thank the witch, but nothing would come out. She drew in a breath, trying to force it past the part of her throat that would create sound, but there was nothing. Just silence.

"Go on then. He's waiting," the witch said and then she sank below the water and was gone.

Standing was a struggle. The bends in her legs—what were they called? She didn't know. Ah well, whatever they were, they wobbled under her, threatening to give out at any moment. The simple kelp dress she'd worn made her feel heavier and more awkward. But somehow, she managed to make it out onto the beach. The waves crashed against the shore, the sound hurting her ears. So loud. Why was everything so much louder on the surface?

"You're late," a deep voice said, accompanied by the sound of something slapping against the wet sand.

Roan lifted her head to look at whoever it was. This must be the man the witch had sent. Fumihiro Jiro. Dark hair, dark eyes, thin, long limbs. He didn't look like he could protect her from the dangers of his world, but then Roan supposed maybe all humans were that gangly looking.

"The spirit said you'd be here two days ago and—" The words stopped in his throat, his dark eyes widening behind his spectacles. "Oh. You're . . . You're uh . . . "

Roan tilted her head in question. She was what? What was she?

"You're beautiful." He cleared his throat, looking away, out to the sea, as if embarrassed. In the silvery light, she couldn't see any traces of a blush on his features, but that didn't mean they weren't there. "She didn't tell me you'd be beautiful."

Roan huffed a breath, rolling her eyes. Beautiful. Like she was some kind of trinket.

Fumihiro Jiro coughed into his fist, nodded to himself, and turned back to her. "We should get you somewhere dry, Roan."

Roan's eyes widened, her mouth falling open. How did he . . . well, she supposed the witch had taken care of that as well. That was likely for the best; he'd need a name for her.

"I'm Fumihiro Jiro." The man held out a hand toward her. "You can call me Jiro."

Roan looked down at the hand, wrinkling her nose.

Jiro watched her for a moment, but when she didn't take his hand, he promptly tucked it back into his pocket. "You don't talk much, do you?"

Roan opened her mouth to snap back at him, but no sound came out, just as before. She huffed in frustration, her hands moving to tap at her throat in explanation.

"Mute? Interesting." Jiro's eyes narrowed thoughtfully, his hands folding behind his back as he leaned forward as if trying to get a better look at her. His brown eyes were sharp, inquisitive, and Roan shrank back from the interest there. "Well, that's a problem for tomorrow. Like I said, we should get you into some dry clothes. Follow me."

He spun on his heel and started back down the beach, the things on his feet slapping against the wet sand. Roan took one step, then another, her legs wobbling under her. Finally, the bends in them gave out entirely, and she flopped down onto the sand. She smacked it in her frustration.

Jiro turned back to see her and rushed back to her side. He reached out his hands slowly, telegraphing his movements like one might with an injured fish. Roan didn't particularly want him to touch her, but there was little choice, and she was getting cold. So, she let him help her to her feet. One warm arm slipped around her waist while the other held her elbow to help guide her across the sand.

"Haven't gotten your sea legs yet?" he joked, a little laugh on his lips.

Roan looked at him through narrowed eyes, wondering if he realized how close he was to the truth.

EIGHT

Irsa

$\mathcal{M}$emories flashed in her mind's eye. Stolen kisses in the dark. Laughter and smiles that Irsa would never get back. There one moment and gone the next. Leaving only the hole where they had been.

"You lied to her." The sea dragon's voice sounded accusing and confused. As if it could not understand why Irsa would make such a sacrifice for someone she didn't know. Slice up and give away piece of herself for a girl who'd never truly understand who Irsa even was to her. "You did not tell her the real price of her humanity."

"It was paid, wasn't it?!" Irsa snapped, pressing the heels of her hands into her eyes as the blackness of the memories threatened to chip away at her mind. What would she be when they were all gone? Would she even be Irsa anymore? When there was nothing of her past left, who would she be? Perhaps it'd have been quicker to kill herself and let Amiphrite reincarnate her as someone else, someone better, someone more worthy of *her*.

"If you do not finish this, how do you know Tynan's

shadow will not haunt you in your next life as well? Will she truly be safe from him?" The creature, seeming to have read her inner turmoil, put words to her fears.

"Stay out of my head!" Irsa whirled to glare at the blank black eyes of the sea dragon. "That was not part of the deal. I gave you permission to go in and take what you wanted to feed the magic; I did not give you permission to read my thoughts! So you just stay out!"

"Apologies, Mistress." It bowed its head as if contrite, but Irsa knew better. The creatures of the Deep did not feel remorse. All they felt was hunger. "It is only . . . "

"What is it?" Irsa snapped, baring her teeth at the little creature. "What do you want now?!"

"We wish to understand why you took the child's voice. It was not necessary for the spell. You did tell her there would be a price, but you could have easily said it was something else, something she would not notice giving up. Why her voice?"

"To protect her," Irsa croaked past the welling emotion in her throat. Taking Roan's voice, it had . . . it had hurt. The child hadn't deserved that. But it was the only protection outside of Fumihiro Jiro that Irsa could think to provide. "Without her voice, she can't easily expose herself."

"Of course." The sea dragon fell silent, bobbing gently in the water beside her.

Irsa swallowed down the upset that had scraped at her throat, squeezing her eyes shut. It didn't matter now. What was done was done. *She* would have approved. For even in her kindness, she had been ruthless. She would have seen that Irsa hadn't had any choice. At least, Irsa hoped she would.

"What is our next course of action, Mistress?"

"We wait."

"Wait? Should we not perhaps go on the offensive? Strike before we are stricken?"

"No. He hasn't even realized she's gone yet. Give him time for that pain to sink in, and then we'll worry about our next attack." Irsa leaned back on her elbows in the sand, watching the magic shimmer around Alon. Tynan was a fool if he thought putting up a barrier would protect him and his from her. "For now, send a few of the smaller creatures into the city, see what's being said."

"Yes, Mistress." The creature bobbed in the water for a moment and then it was gone.

Irsa dug her hands into the sand, pinching it between her fingers. When word spread that the Witch of the Deep had taken the king's own child right from under the guards' noses, the citizens of Alon would be terrified. It was only a matter of time before the tides shifted and their fear turned them against their king.

"WELL, I heard that she ran away," an overconfident gray-tailed teenager said, puffing out her chest as if she were the font of all knowledge. Irsa frowned. Word wasn't really spreading fast enough for her, but it would do. This was just the beginning of the end for Tynan.

"Ah, the certainty of youth." The angler fish's voice was greasy with smugness.

Irsa hated it. She hated how pleased all the creatures of the Deep were with their destruction, but she supposed she wasn't much different. Not anymore.

"You remember what that was like, don't you?" It peered at her through bottomless pits for eyes, drawing back its lips to show off the pointed rows of teeth. "No, I suppose you don't. You've given that up, haven't you?"

Irsa narrowed her eyes, her hands twitching with the desire to reach out and rip the creature fin from fin. Pull out every crooked tooth and leave it bloody for the sharks to find.

"The wards," a jellyfish said, trailing past them.

"The wards," another repeated.

"The wards. The wards. The wards." A chorus of voices as a school of jellyfish hovered in the water, their tentacles leaving soft stinging touches across Irsa's skin.

"What about the wards?" Irsa straightened, her tail already flicking to head off.

"The wards."

"I heard you the first ten times! What about them?" She turned to the angler fish, a snarl on her lips. "What are they talking about?"

"The wards on the drift yard have been breached. Someone is out there." Its voice carried the distinct impression that it did not care that someone was so close to their territory. That someone had swum out into the open ocean without them noticing.

"Who is it?"

"The princess. The princess. The princess. The princess."

"Oh, for the love of Amiphrite, am I to expect every daughter of Tynan this week? All seven of them?!" Irsa groaned, pressing her palms to her ears to try to blot out the voices of the overexcited jellyfish. It did nothing. Their words were in her head, not the water around her. "Which princess?"

No answer.

"Fine. I'll just go and see for myself, shall I?" She swam off in that direction, her hands clenched at her sides. "Honestly, what good is having all these creatures at my command if none of them *do* anything!"

When Irsa approached the drift yard, she found a purple-haired mer floating in the center of the debris, spinning round and round. Her eyes were wild, and her hip-length hair floated around her, winding itself around her body. Irsa wasn't sure what she'd been expecting, but the eldest of Tynan's children hadn't been it.

After a moment of more frantic searching, Fars' eyes finally landed on Irsa. Her shoulders tensed, mouth pressing into a hard line. She had none of her mother's coloring, but still, Irsa could see something of *her* in this girl. In the way Fars held herself, the way she met Irsa's eyes without fear. This girl had the hard edges her mother had had when Irsa had needed them most. This girl would poison someone to protect the people she loved, just as her mother had.

"Your Highness," Irsa said by way of greeting. Pretending not to know Roan had worked in her favor, but there was nothing for it with the eldest. Fars was not naive like her sister. She'd know exactly who she was looking at.

"Witch of the Deep." Fars tilted her head thoughtfully for a moment, then nodded. "You are the one who helped my sister. You gave her the mirror and made sure she could disappear when she ran away."

It wasn't a question, nor was it an accusation. Fars saw these things to be facts, and strangely enough, didn't seem bothered by them.

"Have you come to ask for her safe return?"

"I have not." Fars smiled a little, her lips turning up at the corners.

Irsa blinked, a frown tugging at her own mouth.

"I have come to thank you for protecting my sister, for giving her hope when she had none." Fars' smile spread further up her cheeks, her eyes crinkling with it.

"You believe I helped your sister?" That didn't make

sense. None of that made sense. How could Fars possibly believe that Irsa had helped Roan? Didn't she know who Irsa was? "I'm at war with your father."

"Yes, my *father*. But you've never done anything to hurt myself or my sisters." Fars swam forward, her hands reaching for Irsa's, but Irsa backed away. Even that didn't pull the smile from Fars' lips. "Was I mistaken? Did you hurt my sister? Are you holding her prisoner to hurt Father?"

"No. I wouldn't—" Irsa stopped herself, shaking her head. "I couldn't do that."

"I didn't think so." Fars nodded, pleased with herself. "Then you must have granted her wish. She wished for legs."

"I did." Irsa swallowed down any other words, though they scraped at her throat, begging to get out. More questions than she'd likely ever get answers.

"I knew you would."

"You did?"

Fars nodded, but she didn't answer the unspoken query. How? How had Fars known? How had she realized that Irsa meant her and her sisters no harm? Why did she trust the Witch of the Deep?

"What is it you want, Your Highness?"

"I just want to know that Roan is well. That she's happy and finally free."

"Are you asking me for a way to see her? I can't give you legs too. Your father would boil the sea."

"No." Fars pressed her lips together for a moment, letting out a soft hum. "Not legs. No. I just want to be able to see her. To check in and make sure she's all right from time to time. Could you provide me with that?"

"You wouldn't be able to speak to her." Irsa shifted in the water, her fins flicking. "But I could maybe provide you with a way to see her. It wouldn't be two-way communication, you understand. The water in the air above the surface is too weak to sustain that kind of magic. But I could give you the view from any window or mirror or reflective surface she's near."

"That would be enough."

"Very well. Come back to me in two days, and I'll have the spell ready for you."

"Thank you." Fars bowed deeply at the waist, her hair flowing around her. "Thank you so very much."

Irsa nodded, wrinkling her nose at the bow. "Two days."

"Two days." Fars laughed. She turned to go but hesitated for a moment before adding, "You're exactly how I always imagined you'd be."

Then she swam off quickly, back toward Alon, and Irsa was left frowning at the bubbles in her wake.

"Perhaps you should create a window for yourself, Mistress." A sea dragon poked its snout out from under a bit of broken ship.

"Why would I do that?"

"So you can look after Princess Roan."

"I told you to stop poking around in my head." Irsa's black eyes narrowed on the creature, which had the gall to back away as if contrite. It was one of the younger sea dragons, not the usual creature that came poking around. "You're the little one that's been keeping Roan company when she's out here, aren't you?"

"Yes, Mistress."

She stared at it in silence, watching as it curled its leaf-like fins in on itself, becoming smaller and smaller.

"You care for her."

"So do you, Mistress."

"Very well, I'll let you help me keep an eye on her. We can make sure she's happy."

"Really?" Its fins unfurled as it brightened.

Irsa nodded.

"Thank you, Mistress!"

"Come along then, we have work to do." Irsa spun to head back toward the Jellyfish Forest.

NINE

Roan

---

*R*oan held up a pair of . . . What had Jiro called them? Trousers? She examined them for a moment before holding them up to herself to look at her reflection. She didn't see how they could be very comfortable, but then she was rather used to mermen who wore nothing to cover their tails. Still, these seemed like they would be very restrictive as opposed to the dresses of her people, which flowed around her easily.

"What're you doing?" Jiro asked, his eyes wide as he looked around at all the people staring at them.

Roan's only answer was to hold up the trousers for him to see. She'd think it was perfectly obvious what she was doing. It had been his idea to come and find her some clothes after all. He'd said her dress from home was improper, so she needed some new things.

"You can't wear those," he hissed snatching them from her.

Roan tilted her head in question. She couldn't wear trousers. She couldn't go out at night alone. She had to wear shoes. There seemed to be an awful lot of rules for human women, and she was getting rather sick of being scolded by Jiro.

"This is the men's section." He sighed, lifting a hand to drag down the length of his face. When it reached his chin, he looked calmer. As if he remembered who he was talking to and the fact that she didn't know any better. "Come along, we'll go to the women's section."

She didn't think she cared much for how condescending his tone suddenly sounded, but she was there to learn, wasn't she? She could hardly fault him for trying to teach her, even if he was a horrible teacher. Honestly, he should never ever take teaching as a profession; he'd make all of his students horribly anxious, and probably make himself sick in the process.

"Women usually wear dresses," Jiro murmured out of the corner of his mouth. He was about the same height as her, maybe a minnow or two taller, and she had to wonder if all human men were so short. "The women where you come from wear dresses, right?"

Roan nodded.

"Where *do* you come from?" The question was soft, like he didn't really mean for her to answer it.

Roan pressed her lips into a hard line and rolled her eyes.

"Right. Forgot." Jiro shook his head. "Ah, here we are, the women's department. I'll get someone to help us. You wait here."

He came back a few minutes later with a young blond woman, her hair pinned back into neat waves. Her blue eyes flicked over the dress Jiro had bought for Roan the day before and then she shot Jiro an accusing look.

"Well, there's no accounting for taste in men, is there?" she asked, moving to loop her arm through Roan's and twirling her around to the racks. "We'll definitely find something better for you than that . . . sack he put you in."

Jiro gave a very satisfying sputtering noise, and Roan decided she quite liked this girl.

"I'm Evangeline," the blonde offered, a friendly smile splitting her very red lips. Were they naturally that red? Or had she done something to make them that red, Roan wondered. She'd seen her elder sisters use squid ink to line their eyes, and pinch their cheeks to make them pinker, but she'd never seen anyone use something to paint their lips. She wished she could ask. "What's your name?"

Roan opened her mouth to speak. Nothing came out, and she huffed.

"Her name's Roan," Jiro supplied from where he was trailing them like a guppy. "She's mute."

"Hmmm," Evangeline hummed thoughtfully. "Well, you sit out here, Mister Fumihiro . . . ”

“Fumihiro.”

“Mister Fumihiro, I'm taking Roan to the dressing rooms, and no men are allowed back there. I'm sure you can find something to occupy your time. Perhaps find your *friend* a nice hat."

Evangeline had put a strange emphasis on the word friend, and Roan wasn't sure what that meant. Jiro wasn't exactly her friend, but she didn't know what else she'd call him. Her keeper, maybe. Or caretaker. Not that it mattered. She couldn't say any of those words to correct whatever assumption Evangeline had made.

The door shut behind Evangeline, and her smile dropped. "I need you to be honest with me, can you do that, Roan?"

Roan nodded, her brows pinching together.

"Good." Evangeline nodded to herself, her red fingernails drumming against the door for a moment. Were those painted too? Were they the same kind of paint? They matched. They must be the same. "You really can't speak?"

Roan nodded again.

"That's going to make this a little harder. We'll have to stick to yes or no questions." Evangeline pushed off from the door and moved to sit on the bench along the wall. She patted the space beside her and waited for Roan to sit before taking her hands and giving them a little squeeze. "He didn't do something to you to make it so you couldn't, did he? I mean he doesn't really look the type to hurt anyone, but you can never be too careful."

Roan's eyes widened, and she shook her head, probably too quickly. She wasn't sure where Evangeline had gotten such an idea. Did that kind of thing happen in the human world?

"All right, that's a relief." Evangeline's shoulders lowered, and she gave Roan's hands another little squeeze. "He's not keeping you with him against your will, is he?"

Roan shook her head.

Evangeline narrowed her eyes on Roan, seeming to search for a lie. When she saw none, she relaxed even further. "All right then. Let's find you something fabulous. Shall we?"

Roan wasn't sure what fabulous meant, but the smile that split Evangeline's face told her it must be something good. So she nodded eagerly, a little grin tugging her own lips.

They spent the better part of the next hour going through every dress that Evangeline thought would look good on Roan. In the end, there were so many, Evangeline offered to have them delivered to Roan and Jiro's rooms.

While Jiro paid for her new dresses, Evangeline pulled Roan aside and slipped a little square of paper into her gloved hand.

"I know you said he hasn't hurt you, and that you're here because you want to be . . . " Evangeline's eyes flicked over Roan's shoulder to look at Jiro, her lips pressed into a firm line. "But if that changes, you give me a ring, all right? I know you can't call, but my address is there on the card, and you can always stop by here and ask for me with it."

Roan clenched the card, feeling the edges press into the soft material of her gloves. The gesture was . . . It was . . . Well, it felt like something Fars would do. And all at once, Roan missed her sister. She missed the easy camaraderie, and the way Fars had always looked out for her. She swallowed down the tears and met Evangline's eyes with a blinding smile.

"And you can always come by if you just want someone to talk—" Evangeline stopped herself, flinching a little at the word. "Well, someone to spend time with. I'm sure we'll find some way to chat. Won't we?"

Roan nodded quickly. She reached out to take the other woman's hands and gave them a grateful squeeze.

"You're welcome."

"Roan," Jiro called softly. "It's time to go."

"It was nice meeting you," Evangeline said, giving her hands another squeeze. "I hope you'll come back and let me dress you for the new season."

Roan nodded eagerly, her smile crinkling her eyes.

"Good. And you take care of her, Mister Fumihiro."

"Yes . . . Uh . . . Yes ma'am." Jiro dipped his head, red tinging the tips of his ears. For a moment he shifted his weight on his heels, Evangeline watching every movement through narrowed eyes, then he offered Roan his arm.

With an amused huff, Roan looped her arm through his and let him lead her out of the door.

"Take care, you two!" Evangeline waved from the front

of the store, right up until the door swung shut behind them.

"I think you've just made a friend for life." Jiro bumped his shoulder into hers, a little smile tugging up the corners of hips lips. His spectacles—glasses, he'd called them—slid down his nose a little with the movement, and he had to push them back up.

Roan pulled her gaze from where she'd been taking in the street around them to shoot him a wide-eyed look. A friend for life? But she hadn't even said anything!

"Yes, it seemed Evangeline quite liked you." He nodded. "Even if you couldn't respond verbally to her questions."

Roan felt her lips curling up into a pleased smile again. Her eyes squinted a little with the motion. Jiro stuttered in his steps for a moment, drawing in a quick breath that left him choking and sputtering. Roan reached over to pat his back soothingly.

Jiro took a deep breath, clearing his throat and averting his eyes as he lifted his free hand to rub at them beneath his glasses. "I need to take you back to the rooms for a little bit. I've got to head down to the university library for a few hours to work on some research."

Back to the rooms? Roan frowned at him, her eyes narrowing to show her displeasure at this. She'd spent all of yesterday in the rooms. They'd only been out for a handful of brief hours, and she was not going back to the rooms to just sit. Not again.

"You'll be all right on your—" He stopped when he looked back at her, his eyes widening. His jaw hung open for a moment.

Roan shook her head.

"You're going to find the library terribly boring. There's nothing there for a young woman to entertain herself with."

Roan tightened her hold on his arm, giving his sleeve a

sharp tug. There would be books, and with a little bit of magic, she could read those.

"All right. All right. But don't blame me when you're bored to tears." He huffed, turning down a side street.

THE LIBRARY WAS MASSIVE, bigger than the one in the palace of Alon. Shelves upon shelves disappeared into the depths of the room, each stacked from floor to ceiling with books. Roan's arm slipped from where it had been looped around Jiro's, and her mouth fell slack, eyes wide as a whale's smile.

"I'll just get us a table and—" Jiro stopped, turning back to her with raised brows. And then he laughed, a rich, low, delighted sound. "You like it."

Roan nodded absently, her eyes still fixed on the point in the distance where the shelves seemed to disappear into nothing. How far back did it go? It must be leagues and leagues.

Jiro took her hand, tugging it gently. "Come on, I'll get us a table and find you something to read. What do you want to read about? Art? Music? Or perhaps a novel? What about a magazine?"

Roan wrinkled her nose, trying to think. What *did* she want to read? There were so many books. How could she possibly choose just one?

"I'll get you an assortment then." Jiro picked them a table in a back corner and pulled out a chair for her. "You wait right here."

When Jiro returned, it was with a stack of books tucked under his chin that swayed with his steps. Roan's hands reached eagerly to help him set them onto the table in neat little piles.

"I didn't know what you'd like, so I asked the clerk at the front desk. He said these should interest a young lady." Jiro slid the stack toward her, and Roan tilted her head to look at the spines. Many of them were rather thin. "They're magazines, and a couple romance novels," he said, blushing.

Roan picked one up and flipped it to the front page to read the title, her nose wrinkling a little. Novels were well and good, but they were fiction. She pointed to his two stacks of heavy looking tomes, her brows drawn up in question.

"These? Oh, you won't want these. They're just boring history books. I'm supposed to be doing a paper on—"

Roan plucked the thickest of them from the pile, sending several others skidding across the wood, and opened it to the table of contents.

"Roan, really. That's going to be boring. Give it back." He reached for it, but Roan slid it farther down the table, away from his seeking fingers. He laughed a little, trying again.

Roan shook her head, lifting the book off the table and clutching it closer. It seemed to be a text on early civilizations in a place called Europe.

"If you insist. But I'm going to need that back in a little while." Jiro shrugged, flopping into his seat and pulling out a stack of untidy papers from his satchel. They were all bent at the edges, but he just smoothed them and went digging for something to write with. "I thought you'd be more interested in fun things. Like romance and the latest fashions."

With a thunk, the spine landed on the table, and Roan tapped her finger hard on the bolded letters that read 'History of Humanity.'

Jiro lifted his head to look at what she was pointing at. "Is that why you're here? To learn about humanity?"

Roan nodded, her face splitting into another wide smile.

He blinked, seeming suddenly dazed. "Well, that's a . . . That's a . . . Isn't that something?" He laughed nervously.

Roan nodded again and then ducked her head to her book, wishing she could hide in her hair. But Evangeline had shown her how to pin it back with the hair sticks they'd purchased, and so it was out of her face.

TEN

Irsa

"This feels a little like fraternizing with the enemy, does it not, Mistress?" The elder sea dragon was watching Irsa with something like disdain in its black gaze. The younger—Roan's sea dragon, Irsa had taken to calling it—was bobbing through the water behind her as she worked.

"Fars is not my enemy." Irsa pulled another cracked mirror from the hoard behind her home in the Jellyfish Forest. Why did she have so many cracked mirrors? They were useless for all things except drawing blood.

"She is the daughter of your enemy."

"I believe it was your suggestion that I help Roan by giving her legs. How is this different?"

"Your actions for the princess Roan ultimately hurt the king. It served a purpose. We do not see what purp—"

"And it was your idea," Irsa added, cutting the creature off mid-thought. She tapped her nails against the handle of a mirror.

The elder sea dragon seemed to heave a sigh, its fins jerking out in annoyance. "And it was our idea. But

Mistress, we do not believe you should be wasting magic on something so trivial. Not when the king will no doubt be bringing a war—"

"To our front door. Yes, yes, you've said." Irsa grabbed a small gilded frame. *Finally.* She smiled, running her fingers over the uncracked surface. "I don't think this is trivial. It's driving a wedge further between Tynan and his eldest daughter. His eldest daughter who will inherit when he dies. His eldest daughter who deals with many of the affairs of Alon while her father is colluding with Gavril."

"Very well, Mistress."

"Besides this won't require any of the Deep's magic. I can do this with my own power." She lifted a corner of her tunic to rub against the mirror, wiping away a smudge.

"Of course, Mistress." The creature sounded tired, but it didn't put up any further complaint.

"Are we going to get to see Princess Roan soon?" the younger sea dragon asked, its fins unfurling in its excitement.

"Yes, very soon, little one." Irsa patted the creature's head gently.

"CAN'T I just take it with me?" Fars clutched the mirror between her fingers hard enough to make the glass creak. Irsa's hands twitched with the desire to snatch it away and protect the delicate magic that Fars could ruin with too much pressure. "I won't let anyone see it. I promise."

"It wouldn't be safe in the palace," Irsa said. She'd gone round and round like a whirlpool with the sea dragon over this, and in the end, she'd had to concede that it was right. The mirror could not be within Tynan or Gavril's reach. If they saw where Roan wa, and what she was doing, they could chase after her. She was safest with it hidden.

Still. Fars' eyes had gone large and pleading, and there was so much of *her* in that gesture that it made Irsa's heart clench. Irsa swallowed hard around the feeling, forcing her hand to remain steady as she held it out for the mirror.

"It wouldn't be safe." She was starting to worry she'd have to wrestle the mirror from Fars' fingers. "What if your father or his witch saw?"

"I'll keep it in my rooms, hidden away. No one will even know I have it. I swear." Determination filtered into those pale green eyes, and Irsa felt her resolve slip away into nothing but sand. They were not the same color as *hers*, but they were the same shape, and that look . . . Oh, Irsa had seen that look.

"Very well," Irsa sighed, her hand dropping back to her side. "But no one is to know about this. Not even your other sisters."

Fars nodded firmly. "No one."

She swam away, clutching the mirror to her chest as if it were the most precious thing that she owned.

"You're weak," an octopus muttered, winding its tentacles around Irsa's wrist. "When did you become so weak?"

"I don't think I asked you for your opinion." Irsa jerked her arm from its grasp, ignoring the marks left behind by its suckers. Its colors shifted from brilliant orange to a deep blue, fading into the darkness of the water around them with one final derisive snort.

TYNAN COULD ONLY KEEP the fact that his youngest daughter was missing a secret for so long. Though he seemed determined to keep her disappearance from the general population of Alon, his people were by no means stupid, and it wasn't more than a handful of days before the rumors spread.

"Well, I heard she just ran away. Something about a horrible marriage prospect. Probably that old whale from Stensele. You know he's gone through three young wives in the last century," a young man boasted loudly as he plucked a moss ball from the stack.

"The king would never marry his daughter off to that old manatee. Don't be ridiculous." The old woman behind the market stand rolled her eyes, swatting the vegetable out of his hands.

"I heard it was the Witch of the Deep," a young woman whispered, leaning in closer so that they wouldn't be overheard. "I heard she kidnapped the princess and turned her into a seal."

Irsa clicked her tongue in disgust, dropping the mirror and shoving it away from herself. "Into a seal."

"It is not outside of the realm of possibility." The sea dragon was watching the gossiping mer with rapt attention. "You could have turned her into a selkie."

"Everyone knows selkies were a myth started by the humans to explain the mer they killed. Same with sirens." Irsa rocked back to sprawl out in the water, floating just above the sand.

"Either way, this has brought the king to our door." The sea dragon nodded just over the rock face they were tucked behind.

Irsa didn't need to see it to know that Tynan was approaching with a small army. She had felt them the moment they left the safety of Alon's barrier. The sun glinted off their armor as they moved, casting glares through the water to announce their presence. One would think they'd try to be more discreet. Not Irsa. She'd known

Tynan long enough to know that he was anything but discreet. His whole being revolved around showy acts of dominance that held no substance and which he couldn't back up.

"Pathetic." She let herself drop the last couple of inches onto the sand and sprawled with her hands behind her head lazily. "Shall we go down and meet them, do you think?"

"We cannot see what that would accomplish, Mistress."

"It would accomplish putting the fear of Amiphrite into that bloated puffer fish." She shrugged, closing her eyes so she could let her magic drift across the sands and feel their approach. Twenty men. Tynan had grossly underestimated her. He hadn't even brought Gavril. She wondered if she ought to be offended. "Plus, it'd be rude not to meet His Royal Highness when he has so kindly decided to pay us a visit."

The sea dragon didn't say anything, but she could feel the expression it would have worn if it could. Annoyance. Exasperation. Likely a long, loud sigh. No doubt it thought this would be a waste of magic again. A fleet so small, Irsa likely wouldn't have to call on the Deep at all to defeat them. Maybe that was the little beastie's problem.

"You're no fun." Irsa rolled her eyes, pushing herself up off the sand.

"Apologies, Mistress. We were unaware your conflict against the king of Alon was a game."

"I fail to see what else it could be." She brushed off the back of her fin and moved from behind the rock. "If not a game, what is it?"

"We believe 'war' would be the appropriate term."

"War." Irsa tucked her hands behind her back to force them to stop trembling. War implied bloodshed. She supposed there had been a fair bit of that so far. War, she conceded, was apt.

"Witch of the Deep," Tynan's voice roared through the water, loud and commanding. As if just this sound alone could make her cower.

Irsa swam forward, just close enough so she could see the lines on Tynan's face, before slumping into a lazy slouch. "Tynan, you've gotten old."

"Witch of the Deep," he continued, ignoring her little jab. "I order you to return my daughter to me immediately." His fists clenched at his sides. Power sparked from them, making the water glow with it. Irsa raised a brow at the show of force. Tynan had never been particularly powerful, but with so many refugees within his city walls . . . well. It made sense that he'd be able to draw on their strength if he needed it. Not that it would change anything.

"Return my daughter. Return my daughter. Return my daughter." The words held compulsion, enough that a weaker mer would have hustled to comply. But Irsa was not a weaker mer any longer, and compulsion had long since stopped working on her. Even someone as experienced in it as the elders of the Council wouldn't have been able to force her to do anything she didn't want to now.

The words lashed out toward her, but with a flick of one long tentacle of magic, they were shattered, scattering in the water like plankton.

"You haven't changed at all, have you, Tynan? Ever the overstuffed salamander throwing his weight around and not caring who gets hurt in the process." Irsa tilted her head to one side, a twisted smile slipping onto her lips as the powers of the Deep writhed inside of her, crying for blood. "How many of your own people did you bleed dry of their magic just for that little trick?"

"Is that why you took her? Because you wanted to teach me a lesson? Is that what this is? Vengeance?"

"Tides, you really haven't changed." Irsa rolled her eyes.

"You're just as stupid as I remember."

Irsa saw the movement out of the corner of her eye but didn't turn to follow the progress of the arrow through the water. Before it could reach its zenith, the magic swelled within her, darkness blotting out the writhing, glowing tide of it, veering the arrow off course. One moment it squirmed through the water around her, and the next, twenty thick tentacles shot from her tail and wrapped around the throats of each soldier Tynan had brought with him.

She held out her hand toward Tynan, palm facing upward to the surface, then she squeezed the fingers slowly into a fist.

The soldiers made choking noises, their weapons dropping to the sand uselessly as they scrambled to try to peel the magic away. They squirmed, and writhed, and clawed at the tentacles as their lungs begged for water. Their eyes bulged as her fist tightened the magic around them. Then, one by one, the struggling stopped, until twenty lifeless mer hung before her, limp.

"Pathetic." Irsa clicked her tongue, dropping them. Their bodies drifted upward, buoyant in the shifting tides.

"Are you going to kill me next?" Tynan asked. He hadn't even looked at the bodies of the mer he'd brought with him to die. "Is that what you did to Roan?"

"Roan?" Irsa laughed, the sound reverberating through the open ocean around them, doubling over and over until it sounded as if there were a hundred of her all around them, laughing high and manic. "I didn't kill Roan, I set her free. I helped her escape you. And I'm not going to kill you either, Your Highness. At least . . . not today, anyway."

"Why . . . Why not?" Tynan's hand clenched around the sword at his side, and Irsa wondered idly if he thought he could run it through her. If he thought he could be quick enough to get to her before her magic got to him. They both knew how that would end, but she'd love to see him try. Maybe she'd even let him get close enough to land a blow . . . No. Not today.

"Because I want you to suffer first." Irsa shrugged, then turned her back on him and began to swim back toward the Jellyfish Forest. "Don't bother me again until you decide to take this seriously, Tynan. Next time, I may not be in such a good mood."

"You ought not dismiss me so carelessly," Tynan said through his teeth.

Irsa saw the spark of magic light up the sand around them, pale blue and weak, and had plenty of time to block it or move out of the way. But she didn't bother. She let it land against her back, snapping like a whip, leaving a trail of burning, bloody skin in its wake. She turned just enough to look over her shoulder at him, watching the way his breath heaved, fury turning his face blotchy and pink.

"I believe I just did." She waved her hand, letting a tendril of violet magic sweep out at him, knocking his own power from his grasp, and laying him out flat on his back in the sand. "Go home, Tynan. Before I change my mind."

A trail of blood drifted behind her on her way back home, where the sea dragon waited. It darted around her, fins frantic.

"Mistress, you are bleeding."

"I'm aware."

"Shall we call the jellyfish to administer a numbing agent?"

"Don't bother." She couldn't feel the wound anyway. Why couldn't she feel it? She knew it was there because of the blood that shifted through the water around her, but there was no pain, no feeling of gaping skin, nothing. "It'll close up on its own soon enough."

"Yes, Mistress."

ELEVEN

Roan

That night in the library had been the first of many. Roan and Jiro spent the better part of a month huddled over the table they had claimed as their own amongst the shelves. Every day, Jiro would load their table down with enough books to make the legs creak, and they'd spend hours poring over them. Roan had learned about wars and kingdoms and technology and great works of art. It seemed that Jiro's enthusiasm for humankind was never ending, and she found herself following along on every random tangent he went off on.

"And that's how Napoleon was almost defeated by a swarm of rabbits," Jiro laughed, his hands dropping down to the desk from where they'd been moving with every word he said. He seemed to always be moving his hands when he spoke, much like how the sea witch had woven her magic. Roan couldn't decide if it was distracting or endearing.

She cocked her head in question and held up two fingers like little ears, making her fist hop through the air.

"Yes, that kind of rabbits."

She snickered silently, her hands moving to cover her mouth, eyes squeezing shut.

"You know . . . I bet you've got a great laugh." Jiro leaned back in his chair, shaking his head. "Or you would have, anyway."

Roan shrugged, grabbing the book she'd been reading and hiding her face behind it. She wasn't sure when exactly she'd started turning red when Jiro complimented her, but she didn't care for it one bit. There was too much else to think of now besides his strangely handsome lopsided smiles.

"So . . . I was thinking," Jiro started, reaching over to tap the top of her book so he could get her attention again. Roan peaked out over it, her brows raising. "There's a dig next month, out on the coast. You wouldn't be interested in something like that . . . would you?"

Roan lowered the book, tilting her head in confusion. A dig? What was a dig?

"Right, of course you wouldn't want to do that. Why would you want to go to a smelly camp site and dig around in the dirt for old stuff with a bunch of stuffy intellectuals." He ducked his head, looking back down at his work. "Just forget I said anything."

Roan frowned, shaking her head. That wasn't what she'd meant at all. She set down her book and tapped loudly on the table till he looked up. Once he had, she raised her brows in question again, hoping he'd understand what she meant. Sometimes it seemed that their silent communication worked so well that they didn't need words, but others . . . well, others it seemed they were speaking two entirely different languages.

"I don't know what you're asking me, Roan." Jiro frowned, his shoulders sagging.

Roan huffed, grabbing her book and flipping to the

table of contents. Once there, she pointed at the letter 'w', then 'h', then 'a', carefully spelling out 'what is a dig' with her finger flying across the page.

"What is a—Oh. Oh! Of course you don't know what that means." Jiro laughed. "You know, I should really teach you how to write. That would make this all so much easier."

She thumped the book against the table impatiently.

"Right. Right. So, a dig is where archaeologists go and mine for artifacts. Artifacts meaning items from history. It's . . . Here, let me see if I can find a book." He hopped up and rushed back off to the shelves.

When he returned, his hands were practically shaking with some barely restrained emotion. He had already flipped it open to a page when he dropped it down on top of her own tome.

"This is what it looks like," he said, leaning over her shoulder. He turned the page, pointing to a collection of black-and-white images. "And see, these are the artifacts they found."

A thrill raced through Roan, her heart beating a little faster. This, this is what she wanted. Not just to understand humans of the present but to understand humans of the past. To know where they'd come from and how. Looking up at Jiro, she could see her own excitement reflected in his eyes.

"So, what do you think?"

She opened her mouth to scream, to cheer, to tell him that *yes, yes, she'd love to go on a dig*. But the words got stuck somewhere in her lungs, and she couldn't press them out. The only way left to her to answer was to fling her arms around his neck and pull him into a tight hug.

"I'll take that as a yes," Jiro said, his voice a squeak.

Her hair fell out of its twist as she nodded eagerly.

"Then I'll get the paperwork filed." Jiro pulled himself

away from her, rubbing at the back of his neck. "Till then, why don't I get you some books on the coast, so you know what you're in for?"

He didn't wait for her to answer, just spun on his heel and disappeared into the stacks again, his ears an alarming shade of red.

TRAINS WERE FAST. Faster than holding onto a dolphin as it swam at top speed. Faster than that riptide a few leagues above the drift yard that dragged every bit of debris in a twenty-league radius to it. And trains carried so many more people. Young people. Old people. People in fine suits. People with holes worn into the knees of their trousers. She wondered what sort of mer would ride on a train if they had one in Alon. And where they'd let it take them. Perhaps across the ocean to one of the other kingdoms. Or maybe just to the next town over.

"So, we have to remove the artifact as gently as possible. Some of these things are so old that even the slightest bit of pressure will cause them to crumble," Jiro said. He'd decided to use the train ride to teach her about digs and how best to extract things from the soil. Roan was interested, she really was, and she was trying to pay attention. But the landscape outside the window kept drawing her away.

The glass fogged under her nose where she pressed herself close to watch the colors bleed together through the rain dappled window. It was beautiful. She wondered if she could paint it.

"Roan? Are you listening?" Jiro asked. He sounded slightly amused.

Roan nodded, her head bumping the window.

"No, you're not." Jiro chuckled, the fabric of his overcoat shifting as he leaned forward to peer out the window over her shoulder. "What do you see out there?"

Roan shrugged, her shoulder bumping against his chin.

Jiro hummed thoughtfully, turning his head to look at her wide eyes, then he choked. He seemed to do that quite a lot, choke on air. Roan wondered why human lungs were so fragile that they would choke on what they needed to survive. Coughing, he pulled back and ducked his head back to his book. The shaggy hair that he had taken to wearing in a short tail at the crown of his head fell into his eyes, hiding his face from her.

"We'll be there soon," he said from where he was hiding in the dark locks. "Milo's meeting us at the train station."

Roan tilted her head in question.

"Milo is an old friend from university. He's the one who told me about this dig." Jiro stood to dig through the bag in the carrier over their seats, disrupting the old man beside him in his nap. "Sorry."

The man glared for a moment, then closed his eyes and started snoring again.

Roan snickered silently into the back of her hand.

"Think that's funny, do you?" Jiro asked when he dropped down beside her again with a care-worn journal in his hands.

Roan nodded.

"You probably snore too. We just can't hear it because of your . . . "

Roan's eyes narrowed on him, mouth thinning into a line as her hands fisted in her lap around the fabric of the plaid trousers Evangeline had found for her.

"Oh . . . I didn't mean to . . . Uh . . . I'm sorry. I didn't mean to bring that up." Jiro's eyes had gone soft, pleading. "I'm sorry."

Roan huffed out a breath, short and sharp, her arms crossing over her chest. She had grown to hate her lack of speech. It just made everything harder.

"Look, do you want to see the photos from the last dig I was on with Milo or not?"

Not, Roan thought as loudly as possible and turned her head to look back out the window.

"Suit yourself," Jiro grumbled, pulling his feet up onto the bench in front of himself and hiding behind his journal as he wrote furiously on a page toward the back. They rode on in silence for the rest of the trip.

The train lurched to a sudden stop. Roan jolted forward, her arms swinging wildly to try to keep her balance, but it was no use. She was going to fall. She was going to fall face first on the worn red carpet of the train car. She was probably going to hurt herself. Maybe even break her nose. She was—

Jiro grabbed her by the wrist and pulled, righting her easily on her feet beside him. "I'll get the bags."

Roan nodded, brushing her fingers over her clothes to straighten them. She reached for her little plaid train case; it matched her trousers, as Evangeline had been so kind as to point out.

"Now, just be careful going down the stairs." Jiro gave her a long meaningful look, and they filed out behind the snoring man.

Roan took her time on the stairs, holding onto the railing tightly as her knees wobbled a little. She didn't think she'd ever get used to them. She didn't understand why humans didn't use something else to travel from one floor to another. A sloped floor perhaps.

"Jiro!" a voice shouted through the crowd, and Roan looked up to see a dark hand waving frantically over top of the heads of everyone else. Milo was taller than Jiro by at least a whole trout, and stood above the people around him easily. He had dark skin that crinkled around his eyes where his smile seemed too big for his face. And his black hair fell into his eyes in thick waves.

"Milo!" Jiro shouted back, his voice too close to Roan's ear.

Milo pushed his way through the crowd around him with many a muttered "Excuse me," and then he was in front of Roan, a hand held out to help her down the last of the steps. "Who's your friend, Jiro?"

"Milo, this is Roan," Jiro said, setting their bags down beside him on the damp pavement. "She's going to be joining us on the dig."

Milo's dark brows raised, disappearing into his curly hair. "She is?"

Roan nodded eagerly, turning her hand over in Milo's to shake it, just how Jiro had shown her. A human greeting for a human friend.

Milo's eyes flew from Jiro to Roan, and he let out a soft laugh. "The old goat is going to have a fit."

Roan tilted her head in question, dropping Milo's hand so she could turn her confusion on Jiro.

"He means Professor Hudson. He's a bit of a stickler for the rules. Doesn't want women on digs." Jiro shrugged. "Hudson can stuff it, Lachlan approved it."

Milo shook his head, his lips pressing together as if he were suppressing a laugh. "Of course Lachlan did. All right then, let's get you settled into your rooms. We've got an early start tomorrow."

Roan reached down to take her train case, shaking her head when Jiro tried to take it from her.

"Okay, just mind the sidewalk. It can be a little uneven."

Roan huffed, her chin lifting. She was not a guppy; she

could walk on the sidewalk just fine like everyone else. Her balance was fine these days.

"Car's that way," Milo pointed, and Roan gave him a firm nod before striding off in that direction. Milo chuckled. "Lover's quarrel?"

"What?!" Jiro choked on air again, and Roan found the sound very satisfying. "We aren't—That's not—"

Milo laughed, loud and long, the sound echoing behind her.

TWELVE

Irsa

____

Someone had been there. The wards were undisturbed, and everything looked as it should, but someone had been there. Irsa could feel their magic lingering in the water like oil. And they had taken something. But . . . what was it?

She floated in the middle of her small office, glaring at the shelves. Roan was not the first deal she had made with a desperate mer. There had been the merwoman who wanted to be loved. The merman who needed to win. The wife desperate for a child. The husband who thought his wife was cheating. So many. There had been so many.

Eighteen years of stories, and promises, and sacrifices. Because there had to be sacrifices. Everything came with a price, and her magic did not come cheap. The color of your eyes. Your sense of smell. Your happiest memory. Your saddest memory. All these things and more lined the walls of her small storeroom, making the jars on the shelves hum with their power. She didn't call on their magics often, not wanting to taint them with the darkness required to combat Tynan. But they were there should she ever need them.

"When this is over, I'll set you all free," she said to the shelves upon shelves of glass jars and vials. They didn't answer; they never did. But she made this promise every time. It was a reminder, to herself more than to them, that when Tynan was finished, the people of the sea would be free of Irsa of Tjena once and for all. Whatever that meant.

"None of the other rooms have been touched, Mistress." The sea dragon's fins fluttered in agitation. It disliked the idea of someone in her space as much as she did. Perhaps it was worried what Tynan might find within these walls and how he might use it to wrest control from the depths. That was impossible of course. If such a magic existed, Irsa had never found it. The only way to harness the power of the Deep was to sell your soul to it as Irsa had done.

"Of course not. They knew exactly what they wanted, and it was in this room." Irsa bit at the skin around her thumb nail, eyes narrowed on the shelves. "The question is, what was it?"

"You believe it was someone's bargain, Mistress?"

"Obviously." She jerked her thumb from her mouth when she tasted blood and glared down at the wound she'd just opened. Why hadn't she felt it? Why couldn't she feel anything these days? It had been three weeks since Tynan had shown up at her door, and she hadn't felt anything since he'd lashed her with his magic. No pain. No cold. No warmth. Just . . . nothing. Had he cursed her in some way or was this just another side effect of the magic she used to give Roan legs?

"We really should have re-organized this room for you when we had the chance, Mistress."

"We're not having that argument again," Irsa said absentmindedly. Whoever it had been wouldn't want something small and impersonal. They wouldn't take just anyone's bargain. If they were going to do that, they'd have cleared the storeroom all together. No. They'd want someone . . .

"We know Mistress, but—"

"Roan."

"What?" The sea dragon went eerily still in the water. Only its head turned to look at Irsa.

"They took Roan's voice." The only way to be certain would be to rip every jar off the shelf and check them all, and at well over a hundred, that could take hours. Hours they didn't have.

"Why would they do that?"

"I don't know. But I'm going to find out." Irsa spun in the water, leaving the room behind her and heading down the hall. By the door, she stopped but for a moment to gather her cloak and her satchel, slinging both over her shoulders.

"Mistress! Where are you going? Mistress! We have to reinforce the wards! We have to make sure they don't—"

"We have to warn Fars," Irsa called over her shoulder without a backward glance. Let the pompous little urchin get its fins in a twist. She did not send Roan to the surface just for Tynan and his goons to ruin what little chance at happiness she had. Irsa needed to stop them. Whatever they planned to do. And that started with warning the eldest princess.

Of course, that meant first she'd have to get past the barrier and into the palace without being noticed. But the trouble with Gavril's barrier was that, although it had been constructed to keep Irsa out, it had never really been tested. Tynan foolishly thought his compulsion from eighteen years ago had been strong enough to keep her banished. So they'd added no other protections other than wards to keep her magic from entering the city. Which, admittedly, would pose a problem.

"We won't be able to lend you our power once you are inside, Mistress." The small sea dragon, Roan's sea dragon, warned. Its eyes were watching her worriedly, but it was not making any move to stop her. Good.

"I am aware of that."

"You won't be able to use your own magic either, once you're through the barrier."

"Yes, that will be most inconvenient," Irsa agreed, but she wasn't slowing down. There wasn't time to slow down. She had to get to Fars, and they needed a plan before Tynan and Gavril made their move. "I suppose I'd better not need to use my magic then, aye?"

Roan's sea dragon made an affronted sound.

"What?"

"I'm worried about you, Mistress."

Irsa slowed a little so the creature wasn't pushing itself quite so hard to swim alongside her. She reached out and patted its head gently. "Don't worry about me. I'll be all right. I'm the big bad Witch of the Deep, aren't I?"

"Yes." Its fins curled uncertainly.

"Then there's nothing to worry about." She winked at it and took off again, not waiting for it to follow. There wasn't time for her to sooth every worried creature of the Deep.

The barrier sparked when she got close, seeming to sense her. She floated outside of it, cocking her head to one side. "You aren't going to give me too much trouble, are you?"

Exile. Exile. Exile. The word floated along the current, a faint whisper of the power it had once held against her. Tynan had never even renewed it. The old fool.

"Yes. Yes. Exile. I remember." She laughed softly to herself, narrowing her eyes at the line between open ocean and the city surrounding the palace. "I suppose there is nothing for it. I'll just have to take a swimming start."

She swam back from it a few feet, tightening her cloak around her shoulders, and then took off again, swimming as fast as she could at the barrier. It crackled once, a vague threat of what it could do to her if she didn't stop, but a second later, she slipped through without even noticing. Either she hadn't felt the pain that was meant to be attached to breaking the barrier or there had been none.

"It'd be just like Gavril to make a barrier that was all bark and no bite." Irsa shook her head, pulling her cloak farther up over her short white hair.

The back alleys of the city hadn't changed much since she'd used them to spirit *her* away for their little date to the Jellyfish Forest all those years ago. Nor had they covered up the servant's entrance to the palace. Which was somehow more surprising.

Irsa crept up the long tunnel into the kitchens, her eyes adjusting slowly to the gloom. The noises from the kitchens echoed off the walls, filling the space around her with sound. Then there was a light at the end, the door up into the warm room where mer bustled about, preparing this or that for the royal family. Irsa took a moment to breathe, reaching for her magic just to see if it would answer. It didn't. It remained stubbornly silent.

"Well, if that's how you're going to be, I'll have to get creative."

There were baskets just beside the door full of still wriggling fish and chittering crabs. All waiting their turn to be prepared for His Royal Ugliness. All it took was giving the baskets a little jostle to stir them up and then a quick flick at the clasp keeping them shut. The kitchen was suddenly full of irritated uncooked meals, and in the chaos, it was easy to slip past the staff.

The corridor, it seemed, would provide its own series of problems. Irsa stopped just outside of the kitchens, doing a quick count of the guards again. Six! When had Tynan decided to post six guards in the servants' quarters?

Sending up a silent prayer to Amiphrite that at least her own office may have been left alone, she turned to the left. The passage there was unguarded, and after a couple of twists and turns, she found herself in the abandoned south-east corridor where once she and her soulmate had spent their time. The door to her office creaked loudly in the silence, and Irsa spun to brace herself on the wall just inside, letting out a breath.

"Safe. Now. All I've got to do is find Fars' quarters." Her eyes turned back to the room, and a smile flickered at the corner of her lips. The books. Every single one of them in its place, waiting for her. Every single one humming with the power of the witch she had once been. "Did you miss me?"

They didn't respond. They just sat, waiting. And that was enough of an answer.

"All right then. We've got work to do. Find me the eldest princess." She swam to them, and her fingers tingled where they brushed the spines.

It didn't take nearly as long as it should have, with Gavril's magic woven into the walls of the palace to secure it, to find the princess. The darkness that stained the walls of that wing had been there long before Gavril had even sought a fin-hold in Alon. Long before Tynan had turned his power against it. It was born of love and loss. And it would not be exterminated.

Irsa breathed the darkness in, absorbing as much of it as she could, and followed the whispers of her magic.

Find the princess. Find Princess Fars. Find the princess.

It was older, different from the magic she wielded now, but it still recognized her. Like returning home. It led her down corridors, cloaking her in its darkness from the guards and the servants. When she found Princess Fars, the girl was curled up in the back corner of the library, her head resting on her fist as she read over a stack of papers in front of her.

"You look busy," Irsa murmured, swimming to float on the other side of the table.

"Yes, well, treaties with foreign dignitaries don't write themselves." Fars scribbled something else down on the paper in front of her before she seemed to realize that the person she was speaking to was not who she thought it was. She looked up, eyes widening and mouth falling open, perhaps to shout.

Irsa jolted forward, covering the girl's mouth with her hand. "Shh. I'm not supposed to be here."

Fars mumbled something behind Irsa's hand. It sounded something like, "Yu mst ernly er na."

"What was that?" Irsa pulled her hand away.

"How did you get in here?" Fars asked, her eyes flitting over Irsa's shoulder to check to make sure no one had seen them. "And *why* did you get in here?"

"Roan is in danger. Someone broke into my storeroom and stole her voice."

"Her voice?"

"There's not really time. We have to warn her."

"Warn her how?"

"I need the mirror I made for you." Irsa pulled a book from her satchel, running her thumb over the spine to feel the hum of the magic locked in its pages bleed into her skin. "Then I can find her and hopefully get a message to her."

"So, you *do* know where my daughter is?" Tynan's voice was soft and raspy, like he'd been yelling for the last hour. Irsa didn't startle. She'd known he would find her; it was just a matter of time. She had hoped she'd be able to get a message to Roan first, but it would seem Amiphrite was in no mood to answer her prayers.

"Of course I do." Irsa met Fars' eyes, her chin lifting a little. Fars gave her a pleading look, but Irsa merely smirked before turning to meet the furious gaze of King Tynan. "She's safe. Far away from you."

Turquoise magic whipped through the air, crackling dangerously, and Irsa could have blocked it. She had just enough power left from her books to block it, but she let the blow land. Let it rip open a line across her stomach. Blood fluttered into the water, stringy and metallic.

"Give her back!" Tynan pulled the whip back, readying for another strike. His words broke, almost became a whimper. Irsa had no pity for him. What he'd lost, he'd lost because of his own ignorance. Just like her. "Give her back to me!"

"Why should I?" The words came out through a pant. In spite of the lack of feeling, her lungs still burned with the need for water.

Fars made a soft sound behind Irsa, and Tynan's eyes jumped from the witch to the princess behind her. Irsa moved, putting herself in between them again. Whatever damage he was going to do, he was going to do it to Irsa, not one of *her* children.

"Because I want her back! Because I lov—"

"Don't." Irsa held up her hand, her own power simmering beneath the surface of her skin with rage, begging to be let loose on Tynan. She wouldn't. She'd save it. She'd hoard it away, just in case. "Don't you dare say you love her. You don't. You don't know what love is, Tynan. This is about possession, it always was. It's about control. Roan is not a prized sea horse! You don't own her! Or any of them!"

That was it. That was all it took to make the king snap.

And then he was lashing out at her again. The blows came, sharp and fast, and although she didn't feel the pain, the blood loss made her woozy.

Somewhere off in the distance, she thought she heard her name. The voice sounded so much like *her*, but it couldn't be her. No. It had to be Fars. Or maybe one of the other girls. Larwi. Or Kalah, maybe. Irsa didn't know; she'd never heard their voices. She didn't know how much like their mother they did or did not sound.

THIRTEEN

Roan

oan's hands were not sweating. They were not sweating because she was not nervous. She was not jittery. She had slept just fine the night before. She was not nervous.

"Are you nervous?" Milo asked, a wide smile lighting up his face.

Roan turned to narrow her eyes on him from the passenger seat of the car. He glanced at her out of the corner of his eyes, his smile ticking up a little further.

"Roan's not nervous." Jiro leaned forward to rest his elbows on the back of the bench where she and Milo sat. "She's going to show you exactly how digs are done, right Roan?"

Roan nodded firmly, the corner of her lip twitching into a small smile.

"After all, she did have the best teacher in all of Europe. Didn't you?" He tilted his head, laying it on his folded arms, a grin stretched across his face.

He is terribly handsome like this, Roan thought, and then banished the thought immediately. There was no place in her for it. She had ten months left to enjoy this life; she could not waste it getting caught up in Jiro's riptide.

She rolled her eyes, and Jiro laughed softly, giving her shoulder a familiar nudge. Roan huffed, swatting his hand away, only drawing another delighted little chuckle from him. It may have been annoying, but the gentle ribbing eased some of the anxiety, right up until Milo parked the car in a dirt lot, and they all began to pile out.

Roan wiped her sweating hands on her trousers again, taking a long deep breath. A hand slipped into hers, fingers calloused from book pages and recovering artifacts, giving her hand a gentle squeeze.

"You'll do great," Jiro whispered, then pulled his hand away before anyone could see. She was still mad at him, she told herself, for treating her like a guppy, for telling her she snored, for making fun of her lack of speech.

Roan nodded firmly, lifting her chin and striding after Milo down the worn path toward the dig site. Jiro followed along behind them, whistling softly as he went.

The dig site was . . . It was not what Roan was expecting. Jiro had shown her pictures, and they had almost looked magical, as if the earth was full of artifacts just waiting to be unearthed. People were dirt covered but smiling, showing off the cache of items they'd found. From gold headpieces to whole collections of mostly unbroken pottery. It reminded her of her treasure trove back home in Alon before Father had destroyed it.

But no. This was not that. This was a pit dug into the ground surrounded by string, mud, and flies. So many flies. None of the people were smiling. It smelled like dead earth and sweat. And it was hot enough that she felt the loose hairs from her bun sticking to her neck. This was not magical. This was a mess.

Roan stopped, tilting her head a little.

"Don't worry, it's more fun than it looks," Milo laughed. "Just follow me and we'll find all the best bits. I've got a nose for it."

"Yeah, sure you do." Jiro scoffed, bumping Milo's shoulder. "Don't listen to him. His last big find was a belt buckle. It wasn't even a decade old," he whispered to her, his eyes dancing with amusement. "Come on. Let's look at the list and see where they need us."

He led them to a small canopy with a table set beneath it. Roan turned to watch the small group of men move through the little encampment. Some were in the big hole, clearing earth one small square at a time. Others were on the ground beside it, cleaning things off with little brushes and scribbling away at dirt-stained notebooks.

"Tell me what I'm looking at here, Lachlan," a gruff voice came from somewhere off to the side where a chair had been set up, presumably for whoever was in charge. At least, that had been Roan's experience in Alon: the one in charge got the chair. Like Father and his throne. "Tell me I'm not looking at a woman at my dig."

"That's a woman, sir," Lachlan said, tone flat as his eyes flicked over Roan. Roan didn't turn to look. It was better not to look a shark in the eyes, lest it think you were challenging it. And she had no desire to challenge the older man and be sent back to the hotel when she'd only just gotten there. The dig site smelled, and it wasn't exactly what she'd expected, but she wasn't going to go back now. Not when she was so close to unearthing a little more of what humanity had to offer.

"Why is there a woman on my dig site?"

"It seems she came with Fumihiro and Arturo, sir."

Roan turned back to Jiro and Milo, who were arguing in hushed voices over which quadrant to start on. She reached out and tugged Jiro's sleeve to get his attention.

"What is it, Roan?" Jiro asked, his voice gentle as he turned away from the sign-up sheet to look at her.

Roan jerked her head over her shoulder, gesturing to the older man and Lachlan.

Jiro's gaze flicked to where she indicated, and his face hardened. "Don't worry about Hudson. You got approval to be here."

"Fumihiro, Arturo," Hudson said as he joined them under the canopy. Jiro and Milo moved, flanking her on both sides, each of them lifting their heads to meet Hudson's narrowing gaze. "You brought a woman to a dig site."

"I filed for permission, and it was approved." Jiro's usually smiling face was set into hard lines, his glasses perched high on his nose. He looked every bit the serious professional he ought, instead of the eccentric, excitable boy Roan had gotten to know in the library. It was . . . a strange change. She found she didn't mind it much.

"I didn't approve it." Hudson scoffed. "I'd never approve for a woman to be here. What are her credentials?"

"Excuse me, sir." Lachlan adjusted his own glasses, dark frames almost hiding his round blue eyes.

"What is it, Lachlan?" Hudson's neck wobbled when he was irritated, like a puffer fish getting ready to puff up and scare everyone away. It wouldn't work on Roan; she'd never been afraid of puffer fish.

"This is an open dig, as I recall. Because we were so short staffed, we invited everyone to bring a civilian assistant if they so choose. The only requirement is that they pass the training course and be supervised by one of the staff at all times."

"But she's a woman!"

"The invitation never specified gender, sir. And if she

passes the training course, there is no reason why we shouldn't allow her to participate in the dig."

"She'll be a distraction."

"If she's a distraction, then that's because *you* don't have control of your staff." Jiro's eyes had narrowed into a challenge. His chest puffed out.

Hudson's face turned red.

Roan wanted to step away from him, to put some distance between herself and that anger. She'd seen it one too many times on Father, and she did not need to see it on this man too. But to step back would be to move away from the gentle pressure of Jiro and Milo's shoulders against hers, and she didn't want to lose that. Not yet.

"You can go home too, you ungrateful, puffed up, little—"

"He has a point, sir," Lachlan said. "There is nothing in the paperwork that says we won't accept female assistants, provided they can pass the course. If we were to send her back without even giving her the chance, she would have a case for discrimination. You really don't want the board to hear about this. Do you, sir?"

"No." Hudson deflated. "Fine. She can take the course. But mark my words, she won't last the week. A dig site is no place for a woman!" He shook his fist in the air and turned to stomp off and shout at a few of the men who had stalled in their work to listen to the conversation.

Lachlan met Roan's eyes, his lips twitching into a little grin, and winked. "Good luck, Miss Roan." Then he turned on his heel and followed after Hudson.

"So. Training?" Jiro asked when he turned back to the table. "You have the authority to do that, right Milo?"

"Mhm." Milo dug through the stack of papers on the table until he found a clipboard. "I could pass her right now if you wanted, get this whole thing over with. I'm sure you've already given her enough instruction."

Roan reached for Milo's wrist, squeezing it until he looked at her, and shook her head.

"No? Are you sure? I mean, the faster you get it over with, the faster you get to play in the dirt."

She nodded firmly.

"Jiro?"

"Let's do what she says. Then Hudson won't have any reason to complain. It shouldn't take too long, she's a fast learner." Jiro's smile was back, crinkling his nose.

"All right then. You're with me, pretty lady. We'll see you at lunch, Jiro." Then he headed off to a much smaller pit behind the canopy.

The next several hours were spent in the blazing sun, sweat trickling down her neck, as Milo told her exactly how to extract an item, how to clean it, how to tag it, and how to catalogue it. They went over the process three times, until he handed over the chart and asked her to do it herself.

Jiro joined them for lunch, and Roan watched with fascination as he and Milo joked, laughed, and dug up old stories about previous digs. It was nice. It was almost like being with her sisters again. It made her miss home.

"All right, Miss Roan," Milo said, pulling her from her thoughts. "Show me what you've got."

Roan looked over at where Jiro was sitting on the ground next to Milo, his legs crossed in front of him. A number of the other men had joined them around the small pit where Milo had set up her test, every one of them watching with morbid fascination, like sharks that smelled blood in the water. She shifted on her feet, biting at her lip.

"You can do it. You'll probably be much better than I was at my first dig." Jiro shot her a big, wide smile.

"Oh yeah, you broke your ankle falling into the pit,

didn't you?" someone asked from off to the side, barely containing his laughter. And then they were all laughing and exchanging stories about their worst digs and all the mistakes they had made.

Roan met Jiro's eyes. He gave her a tiny nod, and she knew he was right. She could do this. Warmth spread through her belly, flooding up to her neck like a wave. She nodded back and crouched down in the pit to start the search for the piece of pottery Milo had hidden.

The men were still chattering by the time she unearthed it, digging it out carefully one little bit of earth at a time. She was gentle, long fingers taking their time to work it from the dirt so as not to damage it. And then it was free, and she was brushing it clean and writing it up in the log before presenting the log and the little tray to Milo.

A hush fell over the crowd. Milo picked up the piece, turning it over in his fingers to note if she had damaged it in any way by digging it out. Then he looked over the listing and the tag she'd written and attached.

"Looks good to me. Your notations are a heck of a lot better than Jiro's chicken scratch." Milo nodded. "You pass."

The cheer was deafening.

Jiro moved to the edge of the pit, holding out a hand to help her up. When she took it, he yanked her up into a tight hug, his laughter a breath in her ear. "You did so well."

Roan flushed hotly, hiding her face in his shoulder as she hugged him back. And then there was more whooping and hollering.

"We have to take her out for a first dig dinner!" one of the men shouted.

"Pizza?" another asked with barely restrained excitement.

"Pizza!" they all shouted, and Roan pressed her laughter into the sun-warmed fabric of Jiro's shirt.

❊

BEFORE THE WEEK WAS OUT, Roan was one of them. She worked alongside the men, laughing at their jokes and listening to their stories. She grew used to the smell, and the flies, and the heat. But the excitement that had been there on that first day didn't abate. Every discovery, no matter how small, was met with cheers and this strange human thing called high fives. Roan found herself floating away on the buoyant energy of the people around her.

There was something more though. There were traded smiles with Jiro that lasted longer than they ever had before. There was the brush of his hand when they both reached for the same tool. There was a strange fluttering in her belly.

"Sorry," Jiro muttered for perhaps the third time that day, pulling his hand from the small spade.

Roan shook her head, holding it out to him.

"No, it's all right. I'll use the little pick."

Roan shook her head again, a strand of hair falling into her eyes.

"No, you use it."

She frowned at him.

"Oh, for crying out loud, stop flirting and focus, you two," Milo called from the other side of the pit. The men laughed. Roan ducked her head, a deep blush crawling across her cheeks.

She turned back to her work, ignoring the feeling of Jiro shifting beside her as he moved a little farther into their quadrant. Narrowing her eyes against the glare, she lifted her wrist to wipe the sweat from her forehead. Then the little pick in her hand struck something. Something much harder than the soft clay they'd been working in.

Her gloved fingers brushed against the dirt, wiping it away from whatever had made the soft *clang* of metal on something other than dirt. The dust shifted to reveal a smooth, hard surface. Pottery? Maybe. Or perhaps some kind of tool. Roan held her breath as she worked the dirt away from it, taking small chunks at a time.

"What've you got there, little miss?" Jeffrey asked, peaking over her shoulder.

Roan shrugged, continuing to work.

"Here, let me give you a hand," Jiro said, moving onto his knees beside her. It took them half an hour working together, but in the end, there it was. A large earthen urn, perhaps taller than Roan herself.

Roan looked down at it, her hands shaking. She didn't know what it meant, or what period it was from. One of the men would have to tell her. But she'd discovered it. She'd unearthed it. It was hers in some small way.

"Wow," Jiro whispered. Roan looked up from the pot, eyes widening when she met his gaze. "You're . . . you're, like, really something, aren't you?"

Roan cocked her head.

"Is it okay if I kiss you?"

Roan nodded eagerly and let Jiro pull her in close and press his lips to hers. It was . . . strange and wonderful. Rather like the dig site.

FOURTEEN

Irsa

"You're going to tell me where my daughter is."

The stone of the dungeon was cold. Cold. The first thing Irsa had felt in weeks. Not the pain of the last interaction she'd had with Tynan. Not the tug of the wounds left behind by it. But the cold of the floor she'd been left to sleep on. They hadn't even bothered with a kelp cot or thin seaweed blanket. Just the floor.

"You're going to tell me, witch."

Great Amiphrite, her ears throbbed with the sounds of Tynan's words. Not hurt, just throbbed. Like a low pulse pressing at her ear drums. He was trying to use compulsion on her. Had been trying for . . . How long had it been at that point? A week? Ten days? Not that it mattered. It wouldn't work. He'd never wear her down. She'd take Roan's secret with her to the burial pit if she had to.

"You're going to tell me where my daughter is, Irsa."

"Am I?" Irsa lifted her head from the hard floor to raise her brows at him. A mocking smile twitched at her lips. She wanted to laugh. To flaunt it in his face that he couldn't *make* her do anything anymore. But she was too tired.

"You've been telling me I will for the last . . . How long has it been, Tynan? A week?"

"YOU WILL!"

Irsa snorted, letting her head lull back down to the ground. "I won't. But it's cute that you think I will. Absolutely adorable."

Tynan made a sound like a very annoyed mama manatee, all high pitched and strangled, and flung the door to her cell open. Irsa lifted her head just in time to see the flash of his magic flicker to life and lash out at her like a whip. She thanked Amiphrite for the curse, or the magic, that left her feeling no pain just before the shock overtook her and everything went dark again.

WHEN IRSA WOKE ONCE MORE, the light from outside had faded, and a squat mer was floating outside of the cell.

"You shouldn't provoke him like that. It doesn't do you any good." The mer clicked her tongue, shaking her head.

"It gets him to leave me alone for a couple of hours, doesn't it?"

The door to the cell opened with a soft creak, and the mer knelt on the floor beside Irsa. Faint amber magic lit up the walls as she began to knit Irsa's skin back together, leaving puckered scars in her wake.

"Why don't you just tell him what he wants to know? He only wants to bring the princess home." She shifted her weight back onto her fin, wrinkled hands resting on the bend of her soft yellow tail.

"To this?" Irsa asked, forcing herself to sit up so she could gesture to the walls around her.

"He wouldn't lock her in the dungeons."

"He may as well," Irsa snorted, rolling her eyes. "If he

brings her back here, he'll cage her here. She'll never be free again." The truth of those words tasted bitter on her tongue, making her want to spit to get them out of her mouth. But she didn't. She grit her teeth and reached for that seed of power within her again. It was still there. She had checked every time she passed out to make sure it didn't make the choice to heal her without her notice. She'd need that power when she got her chance to escape.

"It's only going to get worse for you." The mer shook her head, a piece of wiry gray hair falling into her eyes.

"You'd think he'd have better things to do than come down here and bug me all the time. He is king, after all."

"You'd think." The old mer covered a soft laugh with a cough, shaking her head. "Clearly he doesn't."

"Clearly." Irsa stretched her arms above her head, trying to feel the way the newly knit skin shifted, but there was nothing. She couldn't decide if that was better or worse. "Thank you for coming to stitch me up."

"I was under orders."

"Of course. Of course." Irsa flapped her hand through the water, waving the old mer off. "You can go back to whatever it is you normally do now."

She nodded, rising from her place on the floor and heading to the cell door.

"Oh, can I ask you something?" Irsa said, stopping her before she could leave. The mer nodded. "How's Fars? Tynan didn't go after her, did he?"

"No. He doesn't know that you came here specifically to see her." The mer's shoulders had gone tight, her fist white knuckled around the door.

"And you won't tell him, will you?" Irsa's eyes narrowed on the woman. Not a threat, just curiosity. She wasn't sure how, but she felt she knew the answer already.

"I will not risk the princess' life over this petty feud you have with His Royal Highness," she bit out.

"Thank you."

The old mer nodded, and then she was gone. Leaving Irsa to her own devices as she rose to inspect the cell once more. It was an inner palace chamber, likely dug deep into the sand, no windows to the outside that she could use her magic to pry open. There were guards posted at the end of the long hall in front of the only door to the rest of the palace, presumably on the inside and outside. If she escaped, she'd have to deal with them too. And then any other guards she came across. Would she have enough magic for that?

She closed her eyes and reached again, listening to the soft hum of the beast inside. No. There would not be enough. She would likely deplete her stores just getting out of the dungeon. She'd have to wait.

It was full dark when next she woke, the witch light in the hall having burned itself out hours ago. It took a moment to parse what exactly had woken her. With no other prisoners in the dungeon, Irsa had grown used to the quiet. Well . . . perhaps not used to it. It still felt strange to not be surrounded at all times by the voices of the Deep.

But someone was cursing softly on the other side of the door, their voice so low that Irsa could not tell if it was a merman or merwoman.

"Tides! This was much easier when Mother taught me." The whisper was followed by the scraping of something in the lock. A key maybe. No. Not a key.

"Your mother taught you to pick locks?"

The person yelped, whatever they had been using to try

to pick the lock clattering to the stone floor of the dungeons. Irsa pushed herself off the floor, swimming to the door to peek out through the bars at where Fars knelt in front of the door.

"Your Highness?"

"Please don't call me that, Irsa." Fars shook her head, picking up the pins to set back to working on the lock.

"You don't have the key?" Irsa pressed her palms to the rough wood.

"The guards aren't sleeping as deeply as I'd like. I'm not willing to risk waking them by digging through their pockets." Fars huffed. Her fingers twisted the little metal pick she was using in the lock, eyes narrowed on it. "Roan is better at those sleeping charms. Probably because she uses them so often."

"Why are you picking the lock?"

"Because using magic on it would sound Gavril's alarms." Fars' lip was between her teeth. A soft grunt pushed from the back of her throat when she got one of the tumblers to move the way she wanted it to.

Irsa frowned, her nose wrinkling. "Why are you picking the lock?"

"I just told you, because—"

"No. Why are you trying to get me out at all?" Irsa watched Fars' face closely, looking for some kind of answer. What she found was a soft, sad smile and a shake of the girl's head.

"I found Mother's letters. Or . . . your letters, rather. I know what you were to her." She went back to working on the lock as if that was answer enough. It wasn't.

"That doesn't answer the question."

Fars ignored her in favor of focusing on the lock. It took her another couple of minutes to get the tumblers to move in just the right way, then the door sprung open with a soft creak. "There, let's go."

Irsa raised a brow at her, refusing to move. If Tynan found out that her escape had been facilitated by his own daughter, Fars would be in the dungeon herself. Or worse. Maybe Tynan would finally snap and kill one of his own. Irsa didn't think she'd ever see the day, and she didn't want to.

"We have to save Roan," Fars said simply, and that was enough for Irsa.

"How will we get past all the other guards?"

"My sisters are taking care of that. You save what little strength you have left to get out of the city." Fars glided down the corridor, not once looking back to make sure Irsa was following.

"Your sisters?"

"You ask a lot of questions for someone who's being rescued." Fars pushed open the door at the top of the ramp that led down into the dungeons. Four guards were slumped around the wall, leaning against each other as they snored softly. "We need to stay quiet from here on out."

Irsa felt more questions bubbling up in her chest, clawing at her throat, but she nodded. There would be time, later, after, maybe, to ask. To find out how Fars had gotten her sisters involved. To find out what they all knew about her.

There had been so many guards when she'd swum through the palace the first time, lining every hall and blocking every door, but now there were none. And the ones that were around were either sleeping or staring straight ahead as if in a daze. It would seem *her* daughters were far more like her than Irsa had ever thought. A warmth flooded Irsa at the realization. *She* wasn't truly gone, not so long as her daughters lived in Alon. Not so long as they were there, fighting against Tynan and his tyranny.

Irsa would give anything for more time. To get to know the girls. To see what about them they had inherited from their mother, and what about them made individuals. To bask in the parts of *her* that were left. But their trek through the palace was unimpeded, and soon enough, Fars pulled them to a stop beside a crack in the back courtyard's wall.

"This is my stop," Fars said with a forced smile.

Irsa looked at the crack. It was just big enough for her to wriggle through. Then she looked back at Fars. "Your sisters and you . . . "

"We'll be all right. We know how to handle Father. Don't worry about us. You worry about finding Roan and making sure they don't hurt her." Fars took Irsa's hands, giving them a firm squeeze. "Make sure she's happy, for us, won't you?"

Irsa nodded, swallowing around a well of emotion that threatened to cut the water from her lungs. Then she pulled her hands back and moved to the crack to begin wriggling through. She stopped for a moment, her hand pressed to the cold coral wall of the palace courtyards. Cold. Everything was so cold. "I see a lot of her in you. Your mother."

"Really?" Fars wrinkled her nose. "Father always says Roan is the most like her."

"Maybe in looks." Irsa forced the corners of her lips up into something that could almost have been a smile. "But you've got her ruthless streak."

She didn't wait for Fars to say anything else. She turned back to the wall and wriggled through. There was work to do, and no time for reminiscing.

FIFTEEN

Roan

S ome things had changed and others had stayed the same since that kiss. It had been a week, and while Jiro had grown more confident in his casual touches, not much else changed between them. Milo still found them late into the evenings, pouring over the manifest from the dig, working together to identify the artifacts they'd found that day. Jiro still blushed anytime their hands brushed against the same tool. But they smiled more, and Roan found herself at ease in his company more than she ever had before.

"You should just ask her to go on a date," Milo said, his voice too loud, though he seemed to be trying to keep quiet. Roan had learned that he had little volume control. A whisper to him was anyone else's normal speaking voice. And his normal speaking voice was a shout compared to those around him. Roan didn't mind it. He was excitable. That was all.

"I don't think that's a good idea, Milo. She's not . . . We're not . . . " Roan heard Jiro shift his weight on the creaking wooden chair he preferred at the table in their tiny dining room.

"Not what? You don't like her?"

She shouldn't be eavesdropping on them like this. Roan knew that. She knew that it was an invasion of privacy. That if they found out, Jiro would likely be furious with her. But she couldn't seem to help it. Her feet were frozen to the cracked tile floor of the kitchen, the glass of water she'd come out for clutched between whitening fingers.

"It's not that. It's not that at all." Jiro was frowning, she could hear it in his voice.

"Then what is it?"

"I'm going to bed." The chair scraped against the floor. Roan ducked deeper into the dim light of the kitchen, hoping he wouldn't notice her standing there.

"You should ask her. She likes you." Milo followed behind Jiro, clearly not about to give up whatever it was he had in his head. A date. Whatever that word meant. Roan wasn't sure.

Jiro shook his head, making his way into the hall to head toward his bedroom. He stopped, his eyes catching Roan in the yellow light cast by the hallway lamps. "Couldn't sleep?"

She shook her head quickly, hair slipping from her braid to fall into her face.

"Me either. Do you want to work on some more research?" He smiled at her. It was soft around the edges, crinkling his eyes and making him look gentler than she'd ever seen him. Even on that first day when he'd thought she was fragile.

"Research." Milo snorted, perhaps thinking he was being subtle.

Roan's eyes flicked to him, and she pressed her lips together into a thin line.

"Sorry. I'll just . . . I'm going to go to bed." Milo held up his hands, skirting past Jiro toward the bedrooms. "You two have fun with your *research*."

Roan continued to glare after him, even after his door had shut softly behind him.

Jiro laughed, the sound like bubbles in her stomach, floaty and ready to burst. "You scare him, you know?"

Roan shook her head.

"Ignore him. He's being stupid."

He turned back to the dining room, not waiting for her to follow. He knew she would. She didn't have any other choice. She was being pulled into his riptide. She had been, she realized, since that first day.

Roan settled into her normal chair at the table, setting aside her glass of water and pulling a blank sheet of paper to herself. She wasn't sure how to spell the word, but she could sound it out in her head. It would be close enough that he would understand. He always understood. The pen scratched against paper in the silence that had settled over them.

For but a brief second, Roan thought of not asking, but what point would there be in that? It's what she was there for, to learn. She grit her teeth and nodded to herself.

She tapped Jiro on the hand with the pen. He looked up from the book he'd been pretending to pay attention to. "Huh?"

She tapped the paper and shot him a questioning look.

"Oh. Uh . . . A date . . . " He colored. "It's when two people who fancy each other go out to dinner, or on a walk in the park, or to the cinema, or dancing, or something."

Roan nodded her understanding and then tapped the paper again, more pointedly this time. He would under-stand. She knew he would.

"Are you asking me on a . . . ?"

Roan smiled.

"Oh." The red had stained all the way down his cheeks, working its way toward his neck. "Yes. I'd like that."

Roan ducked her head, hiding in her hair. She'd like that too. She knew she would. Even if she didn't know all of what it would entail, spending some time with just Jiro again after so long on the dig would be nice.

"This weekend. Saturday. We have the day off from the dig. We can go then?"

Roan nodded eagerly.

"Dancing, maybe? You've never been dancing, have you?"

Roan shook her head.

"Great. Then you won't realize how bad I am at it." Jiro laughed, and Roan joined him, letting a feeling of warmth wash over her. He fancied her. Now . . . she just needed to find out what that meant exactly.

THE NEXT DAY dawned too bright and too early, but neither that nor the crick in her neck from the flat pillow could belie Roan's mood. She had just five days of the dig to get through before her date. Jiro liked her, fancied her, likely in a way that was more than friendly, if the conversation between him and Milo was anything to go by. She'd have to confront Milo about that sometime later. And she had a full day at the dig site ahead of her. It would be a good day. The best day!

One breakfast of overcooked porridge—thanks to Jiro —a quick shower, and a drive to the dig later found Roan staring at . . .

Well, she wasn't really sure what she was staring at.

Or who, rather.

There was something oddly familiar about the raven-haired woman who was up to her ankles in mud from the previous night's rainfall, her dark hair swept back in a tight bun, a serene smile on her face. The men crowded around the pit where she was working, murmuring excitedly to each other.

"Milo! Jiro! You have to see this. Sabrina has found a whole slew of tools!" Francis shouted, his eyes wild with excitement. Jiro and Milo made their way over to the pit to look at what they'd discovered, and Roan found herself swept up in the tide.

"Cobbler's tools, it looks like," Sabrina said, her voice soft but confident. And oddly familiar, just like her face.

"Oh, of course! You're right, they are cobbler's tools!" Jeffrey laughed. He took the tray from her and started tagging the items.

"You must be the other girl on the dig." Sabrina stood, brushing dirt off the knees of her meticulously pressed trousers. "Roan, right?"

Roan nodded. She held out her hand to the other woman, just like Jiro had taught her.

"Sabrina." Sabrina took her hand and gave it a dainty little shake before dropping it. "Lachlan told me there would be another girl around. It'll be nice not being the only one. I look forward to getting to know you."

Roan offered the woman what she hoped was an encouraging smile and nodded again.

"And who are these handsome lads you brought with you?" Sabrina turned to Jiro and Milo. The pair stopped looking over the tools and turned toward her voice, eyes wide. "You must be Fumihiro and Arturo. Hudson told me you two were the best there is."

"Hudson said that?" Milo asked, wrinkling his nose.

Jiro laughed—an octave higher than normal. Roan

turned to see that his ears had turned a startling shade of red, and her stomach dropped. "I don't know about the best. But we're pretty good."

"Pretty good? I read your paper on hieroglyphics versus the modern writing system. The evolutionary patterns you found were startlingly genius."

"Well . . . ancient languages are my specialty." Jiro rubbed the back of his neck.

"I'd love to pick your brain." Sabrina's face had split into a wide smile, her dark eyes glittering.

"Oh, umm . . . sure? How about . . . how about we go grab some coffee?" Jiro hooked his thumb over his shoulder in the direction of the tent where several other men were milling about drinking tin cups of stale coffee.

"Perfect." Sabrina held out her hand to him, and he pulled her from the pit. Once she was on her feet, she looped her arm through Jiro's and let him guide her toward the mess tent.

Roan stood, blinking after them, her boots slowly sinking into the mud.

"Don't worry about it, Roan," Milo said, bumping her lightly with his shoulder. "He just gets all flustered when people have read his work."

Roan nodded, not having the words to identify the feelings swimming through her, nor to explain why she was feeling them. There was no reason for her to be upset. No reason for her stomach to be dropping down to her feet like an anchor. No reason for the corners of her eyes to be burning with unshed tears. None at all. And yet, her body seemed to be reacting to something she couldn't quite understand.

"Come on, let's get to work. He'll be back with us soon."

Roan let Milo lead her back to the pit. She let herself fall back into the steady flow of their work. It was easy. The repetition of dirt beneath her spade as she dug away at their quadrant let her mind drift. Let herself forget, if just for a moment, that there was something very wrong with her.

"Sabrina has decided to join us. Hudson says someone has to supervise her, just like Roan, so I thought Milo and I could handle it. That's all right, isn't it?" Jiro asked, his hand wrapped around a tin mug of tea. He held it out to Roan, his eyes wide and hopeful. "It'll be nice to make another friend, right?"

Roan wanted to say no. She wanted to smack the mug from his hand and send it clattering to the ground. She didn't do either of those things. Not that she could explain what stayed her hand, other than that Jiro's eyes were so soft behind his glasses, a smile twitching at his lips, that she couldn't say no.

So, she nodded. And Sabrina joined their ranks.

"It'll be fine," Milo said under his breath, his tone surprisingly quiet.

IT WAS NOT FINE. At least not as far as Roan was concerned. Sabrina spent the rest of the day hanging on Jiro's every word like a barnacle, which was bad enough. But what was worse was that she could talk back. She could share her own theories. She could engage him in friendly debate. She could . . . do all the things Roan couldn't do without a voice. And every time she laughed, something prickled at the back of Roan's neck, a familiarity she didn't understand.

"So then she said that she'd learned Japanese as a way to better understand the flow of ancient Chinese poetry. Can you imagine? She knows Japanese and Mandarin? Isn't that just . . . " Jiro sighed, leaning back in his chair.

Roan slammed the book she'd been reading onto the table, making their teacups clatter softly. Milo looked up, but Jiro didn't seem to notice. He was too caught up in whatever he'd been saying, his eyes far away and distant, a faint flush staining his cheek.

"We're going to the museum on Saturday. It's going to be so much fun. I just . . . She's really something, isn't she, Milo?"

You're . . . you're, like, really something, aren't you? He'd said that about her not but a week ago! That *she* was really something. Roan stood from her chair and stomped down the hall toward her bedroom.

"What's gotten into her?"

Milo didn't say anything, but Roan could feel the weight of his stare on his friend. She grabbed her hat, stuffing it down on her head, slung a little purse over her shoulder, then headed for the door.

"Roan? Where are you going?" Jiro rose from his chair, perhaps to follow her.

"Let her be, Jiro. She probably just needs some air." Milo grabbed his arm, stopping him.

Air. That's exactly what she needed. Fresh and briny. Tinged with the soft rumble of the tides. Sand gritting between her toes. She needed . . . she needed the sea.

Roan slammed the door behind her.

SIXTEEN

Irsa

_S_omeone was calling for her. They were not using her name, and she could not hear them, but they were calling for her. Irsa knew they were.

"We should have returned to the forest," the sea dragon said disapprovingly from where it floated at her side.

"We weren't safe there." Irsa ran a hand through her hair, trying to focus through the incessant call. She'd have to go to it. No matter how she tried to avoid it, she'd have to go to it. She couldn't leave Roan alone, calling into the sea for someone who never came.

"We were safer there than here. Here, we are exposed."

Irsa's eyes swept the drift yard through the window of the one mostly intact ship they had found. It was not ideal, that was true. It would be easy for them to be surrounded there. But there were no other options. They couldn't go back to the forest, not yet. Not when she had no way of knowing what sort of traps Gavril had set up there in her absence.

"If you don't like it, you can leave." Irsa's fingers

twitched where they were slowly weaving a new set of wards for their little hideout. Her nose was bleeding; she wasn't sure when it had started. She didn't think it mattered. Not now. The power of the Deep had flooded back into her the moment she'd left Gavril's barriers, and now every time she used it, her head swam. "You all should stay here. The wards will protect you until I get back."

"Back from where?" an angler fish, whose light was wobbling ominously in the corner, asked.

Irsa didn't bother to answer. It would change nothing. They wouldn't convince her not to go, no matter how dangerous it was. Roan needed her. "I shouldn't be long."

"Where are you going?" The sea dragon sounded annoyed, which was a stretch for such a toneless creature.

"Out." Irsa finished, letting the blanket of her magic layer over the entire drift yard to protect the beasts within. She wasn't sure why she was bothering; they could all protect themselves, or just go back to the Deep to hide if they had to. She smeared the blood under her nose with the back of her hand, sniffing a little.

Her hands twitched to gather supplies. To throw what little weaponry she had available to her into a bag to take along. But there was nothing. Every bottled spell. Every book. Every cursed item. They were all at her home in the Jellyfish Forest and she was not willing to risk going back there. Not yet anyway.

"You're still weak, Mistress."

"I'm fine." She'd just have to hope the magic was enough. It always had been before. But that had been before. Before she'd gone days without it coursing through her veins and let Tynan brutalize her over and over again. Before she'd lost all that blood. Amiphrite, she'd lost so much blood.

"You're bleeding." The sea dragon did not sound amused or even sympathetic.

Irsa ran her wrist below her nose again, smearing the blood up her arm. Thank Amiphrite the wards would keep the sharks away. "I'm *fine*."

The sea dragon made a noise that might have been a derisive snort.

Irsa rolled her eyes. She was running out of time. The call was getting more desperate. "I don't have time to argue with you."

"Of course not."

She swam through the opening where a door might have once been and out into the open water, not bothering to acknowledge the feeling of disapproval from the creatures of the Deep. It had been their idea to help Roan in the first place. She was just doing as they'd suggested.

"You're off to see Princess Roan, aren't you, Mistress?" Roan's sea dragon asked, its fins jittering excitedly as it kept pace with her.

"I am."

"I'm coming with you."

"I don't see where that will help, but sure." Irsa shrugged. She held out the satchel at her side. "It'll be a long trip on the stream. You should hop in."

"Right!" The little creature buried itself in the soft seal leather, and they were off. Following the call was the easy part. The jet stream spat them out less than a league from the beach the call was coming from.

"She's so unhappy," the creature said, poking its head from the bag.

"It might not be something serious. She is a child, after all." Irsa wasn't sure if she was trying to convince herself or the little creature more. Either way, it was a lie. Roan wasn't just unhappy. The call she'd sent out was the wailing sound of heartbreak. It was the sound of a child who had loved and lost. It was . . . It was the end, Irsa realized. Roan would want to come home.

"I don't know, Mistress."

"We should go up to the surface. See if we can figure out where exactly it's coming from."

The call was drowning out everything else she could feel. All there was was the clenching feeling of heartbreak and loss. The lack of understanding of how this could have happened. Roan couldn't be far.

"Is that safe, Mistress?"

"Do we have much other choice?"

The sea dragon blinked at her slowly. It probably would have been frowning if it could. Either way, she was right, they both knew that she was. "You stay here. I'll just go and have a look."

She didn't wait for it to reply, her fins flapping behind her toward the surface. The sky above was clear, the moon casting the beach in a soft glow, lighting Irsa's way. And there, her feet ankle deep in the waves, was Roan. Red hair thrown over her shoulder in a sloppy braid, thin pants soaking up the water as it flowed around her.

Roan's expression was shadowed by her hair. Irsa pushed herself closer, focus intent on the girl standing on the unfamiliar beach. She needed to know that Roan was all right. And if she wasn't, Irsa would do whatever was within her power to make it so. She would boil the seas if the need arose.

Pain shot through her, sharp and violent. The first pain she'd felt in weeks. Irsa winced, her vision going dark for a moment. She blinked down at where the pain had origi-nated. An arrow had buried itself into her shoulder, deep enough that she could almost see it on the other side.

"Not a bit further, witch," someone hissed. She followed the rope attached to the arrow through the water, and there, swimming a short distance away, was one of Tynan's mer.

Irsa's fins whipped, pushing her closer to the beach. She was almost there, almost within hearing range, she was sure. If she could just get a bit closer.

"I said, no further!" Heat shot through the rope, burning at the skin around the arrow and everything inside.

Irsa screamed, the sound ripped from her throat as her vision blurred with tears. Pain. So much pain. Why was she feeling it now? Why hadn't she before? But Roan. Roan needed her. Something wrapped around her—the rope, she realized. The coarse material chafed at her skin.

"Bring her this way," Gavril said, motioning for the guard to drag her along through the water.

They were getting closer, almost close enough to Roan that Irsa could shout and get her attention. She opened her mouth to call out, to warn Roan to run, to go back to the land and stay there.

Gavril grabbed her throat, his magic cutting off the breath she'd need to make a sound. "I don't think so. You say a word to that girl, and I'll kill her. I don't care what Tynan says, she's not worth all this trouble."

"Why bother with her?" Irsa pressed the words out through his magic, voice strangled. "You've got me right here. Finish me off. That's what he wants. Kill me, and we can be done with this, all of it. Let her go."

Gavril laughed, the sound like teeth on coral. "Because that's not what I want, Irsa. This was never about Tynan. Or his children and wife. Or you, for that matter."

"Then what's it about?" Irsa wondered if she could distract him long enough to keep him from going after Roan. Maybe she'd go back inland when it seemed she hadn't reached anyone with her call. She just had to keep him talking. She just had to stay conscious through the burn of the arrow in her shoulder melting away muscle and ligaments. She may never be able to use it again, not after this.

"It's about me, of course." Gavril tilted his head back, an arrogant smile cutting across his face like a knife.

"You?" Irsa snorted, rolling her eyes. "How is all this about you?"

"Oh, little Irsa. All of this has always been about power. Tynan is so consumed with your little fin measuring match he doesn't even notice what I'm up to half the time." Gavril shook his head, his tongue clicking as if in sympathy. "Now, if you'll excuse me, I have a princess to comfort. Don't forget: you scream, she dies."

He didn't wait for her to answer or nod her understanding. He swam toward the beach, letting the dull moonlight filter over his dark hair. Roan looked up, sniffling loudly, her eyes glassy. Heartbreak, that was the expression Irsa couldn't make out before. She could see it now, this close up. Her hands twitched to reach out to the girl, to comfort her in the way her mother might have. The arrow pulsed with another round of searing pain.

Roan's eyes widened at the sight of Gavril. Her head shook as she backed away from him, hands up to ward him off. Gavril stopped, just close enough in the water that he could remain nearly to eye to eye but still be heard.

"Come now, princess, I'm not here to hurt you." Gavril's voice was soft and leading, tinged with just enough compulsion to make Roan stop in her tracks but not enough for her to notice he'd used it. This, Irsa realized, was Gavril's true potential, his true danger. He was quiet and unassuming. Handsome and disarming. They would not know what he was up to until it was too late. "Are you here looking for the witch? The one you met at the drift yard?"

Roan nodded in answer without any hesitation. Irsa groaned softly, the sound burning her throat. Roan was naive and foolish, so unlike her mother, who would have seen through the ruse the moment Gavril appeared. Who would have turned Gavril's own compulsion back against him. She'd been just enough like her mother to be adventurous and spirited, but she'd not gotten the viciousness as Fars had.

"Oh, Roan." Gavril sighed, soft and sad. "You don't know, do you?"

Roan's head tilted, confusion making a wrinkle appear between her brows.

Gavril shook his head, tutting softly. "Sweet, innocent girl. That was the Witch of the Deep. She cursed you, didn't she? She took your voice and sent you to run about on land without it?"

Roan's shoulders stiffened, her chin tilting back. She didn't say it, but Irsa could see a little of her mother's anger in that motion. A little of the defensiveness that had led her mother to protect Irsa with everything she had. If only Irsa had been able to do the same. If only she could do the same now, protect her child. But the ropes hissed with heat, her skin blistering beneath them, and already her vision was closing in to a pinprick. No. She had to stay awake.

"Oh, you thought she was granting your wish. Didn't you?" Gavril frowned. "You thought she did this to help you?"

Roan nodded slowly, as if testing the words.

Gavril sighed, his hand moving to his chest as if he were the one in pain. "No. She did this to hurt your father, and to hurt you. Who do you think that girl is who has your voice?"

Roan's head shot up, her eyes wide, mouth falling open.

No. No! Irsa thrashed against her bonds, ignoring how

the skin beneath them had started to rip. Reaching for the power of the depths to sing through her veins. But there was something blocking it. Gavril hadn't just tied her up, he'd choked off everything she needed to save herself. To help Roan. To tell the princess the truth! She had to tell her the truth! That Gavril had stolen Roan's voice. That it was one of his people. That Irsa would never, *could* never do that to her.

"That's right. It's Irsa." Gavril's tone had gone soft, gentle, and pained. Like he didn't want to be the one to have to tell Roan this but he knew he had to.

Roan gasped, stumbling back from the words. Her hat fell from her head to expose eyes glittering with tears. And then she was running, not away but into the water, the sea splashing up onto her clothes and dragging them down around her. She grasped Gavril's hands once she reached him, the waves now up to her waist.

"What? What is it, princess?" Gavril's tone was full of faux surprise and misunderstanding. He knew what Roan wanted now. He just needed her to ask for it. That was the rule of magic like this: the person had to ask for it. Just as Roan had to ask for her legs, she'd have to ask for her fins too. She'd have to ask for her deal with the Witch of the Deep to be broken.

Roan pointed desperately back toward the ocean from where Gavril had come, her hands shaking. Irsa fought against the ropes. If she could just get free. If she could just get to them in time to explain. Roan could take it back before Gavril —

"You wish to come home now, princess?" Victory lined his tone.

Roan nodded.

"NO!" Irsa screamed. The magic still bound her, searing

into her skin enough to melt it. But it was too late. And as the light of Gavril's magic rose around them, Irsa lost her battle with the pain, and the world went dark.

SEVENTEEN

Roan

There was a scream. A scream that was not her own. Roan knew it was not her own because in spite of her legs knitting back together, the skin melting and the bones breaking and reforming, she had not regained her voice. Her deal with the Witch of the Deep was null, but she had not regained her voice. She had wanted to scream; her throat had gone raw with the feeling of needing to. But no sound would leave it. Or more accurately, there was no sound *to* leave it. Still, she could hear someone screaming, sobbing, shouting, "No!" over and over.

It was worse, Roan thought. Legs to fins was worse than fins to legs. Was it because of the excitement that having legs had brought? Was it because a return to her fins meant an end to her dreams? Was it the way her heart felt heavy and leaden in her chest? She couldn't tell. All she remembered was thinking, *Oh, this is worse,* before the pain took not just her chances at adventure and understanding humanity but also her consciousness.

The bed beneath her was soft when she woke. Not lumpy like the one in the apartment she shared with Jiro and Milo. The air was thicker . . . No, not air. Water. It was water she was breathing in, briny and fresh. The sea. She was back beneath the sea. She was in Alon. The night on the beach where she had traded her legs for fins again had not been a dream.

She sat up in bed, her fingers moving to rub at her throat. It was sore, scraped raw by tears and unspoken screams. Roan opened her mouth to test her voice, to see if it had returned, but nothing came from it. Not even the soft vibrations of muffled sound. Letting out a sigh, she threw the blanket off of her fin.

The door to her room opened, admitting one of the maids with an arm full of clothes. She stopped at the sight of Roan, her brows raising. "Oh, Your Highness, you shouldn't be out of bed yet. You've been through an ordeal. His Majesty wants you to rest for at least another day before you meet with your fiancé."

Her *what*?! Roan's head jerked up, her eyes widening at the other woman.

"Lord Gavril was quite understanding, of course," the mer chattered, seeming not to notice the bewildered expression. "You know, I never thought much of him before. But the way he was carrying you when he came back . . . Well, if you don't mind me saying, Your Highness, it was very romantic. Dashing, really."

Roan frowned. That was to be her punishment, she supposed. She had gone against Father and run away, and he had wasted no time in finding her a husband. No doubt Gavril would tie her to him in such a way that she would never escape again.

"Oh, don't look so sad, Your Highness. I'm sure you'll get to see him soon. Everyone knows how he rescued you. His Majesty can't possibly keep you apart for long."

Rescued. Yes, that would be a better story, wouldn't it?

To think she had been kidnapped, and tricked, and used, instead of that she had run away of her own free will. Father wouldn't want people to know the truth of it, and Gavril, of course, would be more than willing to go along with the lie. So long as it furthered their agenda against the Witch of the Deep.

"And that witch." The maid shook her head, pulling a dress from the pile on the chair to hang in the wardrobe. "Well, she'll be gone soon anyway. I'm sure of that."

That should have been a relief, Roan supposed. To know that the Witch of the Deep would be gone. To know that the woman who had taken the first love she'd ever known and twisted it as she had would suffer for what she'd done. But it didn't. There was no satisfaction in vengeance. It left her feeling hollow.

"Ah, but look how beautiful these new gowns Lord Gavril chose for you are!" the maid said, her tone full of forced cheer. "I mean this . . . this purple one will look lovely with your complexion."

Roan nodded. She supposed it would. Maybe that was the one she'd wear when she met with Gavril. Or maybe it would be another from the truly impressive stack of jellyfish silks and seaweed taffetas. Just not today. She would not meet with him today. Roan entertained the idea of lying in bed and playing up whatever perceived trauma Father had told everyone she'd suffered from. Her fins did ache, after all, and it would be far easier than facing the world. But she had made a promise to Fars.

She rose from the bed, stretching out her fins to relieve some of the stiffness. How long had it been? How long since she had returned to Alon? Did Jiro miss her?

No. She wouldn't think of him. She wouldn't think of that, of the life she'd left behind. Not when there was a future ahead of her here. Perhaps not a future she had planned nor wanted but a future all the same. A future she was . . . resigned to, she realized. It would be easy to be Gavril's now. She felt numb to the idea, neither disliking nor enjoying it. She would be provided for. She would not have to leave home and her sisters behind, as she had always worried she would. It was the best of a bad set of solutions.

"Your Highness, you can't just get up like that. The healer said you should stay in bed for at least another day," the maid was saying, swimming to Roan's side to try to push her back down onto the bed by a gentle press of her shoulders.

Roan shook her head, brushing the mer's hands off of her. She had to see her sisters. She had to tell them about where she'd been, and who she'd met, and all she'd seen. She had a promise to keep.

"Your Highness."

Roan swam to the wardrobe where the mer had been hanging up her gowns and pulled a deep blue one from the lot. One of her favorites: crushed seal velvet that sat high up on her neck and stretched to cover her wrists. It had been one of Fars' old gowns. It was a comfort. A small one. Perhaps the only one she'd be allowed to have now that everything else was ruined.

"Your Highness, that's hardly proper to be wearing to see your betrothed." But the maid didn't stop her as Roan pulled her ruined pajamas over her head, discarding them on the bed, and yanked the dress on. Of that, Roan was grateful. "I'll just get rid of those for you, shall I?"

Roan's hand reached out and grabbed the mer's wrist before she could second guess the notion. She squeezed once, hard enough to send a message, meeting the maid's gaze. She shook her head.

"Oh . . . If you say so, Your Highness. I'll just . . . I'll put them in a drawer?"

A nod, then Roan turned back to the matter at hand: her hair.

AFTER AN HOUR of struggling with her red locks, Roan had finally managed to corral it into a braid that looked marginally respectable. The maid had left at some point, and in the silence, Roan felt the weight if the sea on her shoulders. She took a breath, lifted her chin, and pushed them back. There was no time for self-pity.

The guards outside her door looked at her as if they might try to stop her from leaving her rooms, but they didn't. She didn't let herself linger too long on the strangeness of that. In fact, none of the guards stopped her in the halls on her way to Fars' quarters. They merely watched her, posture erect, eyes alert.

There was a seal on Fars' door. It glowed with the harsh electricity of Father's magic. Roan lifted her fingers, hesitant as she reached for it, but it didn't seem to react to her touch at all. She knocked.

A creak, and the door opened to reveal another set of guards on the inside of Fars' small sitting room.

"You should be in bed, Princess Roan," one of them said, his tone that of a man on the verge of grabbing her by the arm and dragging her back there himself.

"Let my sister in." Fars' voice sounded strange. The guard looked at her over his shoulder, his mouth opening to say something in return, but Fars cut him off. "I am not permitted to leave my quarters, but Father never said anything about me not being permitted visitors."

"Yes, Your Highness." He moved out of Roan's way, his mouth pressed into a firm line.

"You may wait in the hall."

"We are under orders—"

"You are under orders to ensure I don't leave my rooms. The doors and windows have been sealed with my father's magic. There are guards posted outside of both. How, might I ask, do you think my sister and I will escape with such precautions in place? Or do you think that my father's magic and his men aren't capable of keeping us in place?"

"We'll be outside," the other guard said, taking the lead and expecting his partner to follow. The door shut behind them with a soft click and the crackle of Father's magic sealing them inside.

Fars finally lifted herself from where she'd been sitting in the shadow of a witch light and made her way over to Roan. She looked tired and hollowed out, her cheekbones more pronounced than ever before, and her scales showing none of their usual shimmer. Roan frowned, reaching for her sister, pulling her in close.

"Don't worry about me, Roan," Fars said, but she let herself be pulled into Roan's embrace. She held on as Roan pushed them to the small, tufted seal leather sofa in the corner. She allowed Roan to pull the blanket from the back and drape it over her shoulders.

"Stop fussing over me." Fars shooed Roan's hands away as she went to tighten the blanket further. "I'm fine."

Roan stared at her, blinking.

"There are more important things than this." Fars' eyes had gone hard. She took Roan's hands, giving them a firm squeeze. "Much more important things."

Roan nodded and rose to head to the little writing desk along the wall, pulling paper and an inkwell from it. Of course, Fars would want the story of what had happened. She'd want to know all that Roan had seen. It would take some time for her to write it all out. It was too easy to fall back into this mode of communication. To write out her thoughts as she had been with Jiro and Milo for the last several weeks.

Fars reached out and took the pen from her hand. "Not that. That can wait."

Roan frowned.

"You have to go and find Irsa."

Irsa? Roan's head tilted.

"The Witch of the Deep."

Roan's expression fell, hardened, as pain gripped her chest. Why would Fars suggest that? Why would she—

"Your human is in danger. Gavril has plans to kill him before your wedding."

She hadn't eaten anything since dinner that evening with Jiro and Milo. She didn't know how long ago that had been, likely days at the very least. Even still, she felt her stomach jolt and gurgle, threatening to bring back up anything that might have lingered in it. Her hands shook as she a wrote single word onto the pad pressed against her bent tail.

Why?

Fars sighed, fingers reaching to brush a strand of hair back from Roan's face. Her touch was gentle, kind. Like she knew what she was about to say was going to hurt. Just how it had when Roan's first seahorse had died.

"That human is your soulmate."

She'd been right, it did hurt. It hurt like an ache, starting in the bones of her hands and spreading until it reached every part of her, making her sit frozen, the pen floating to the floor and rolling beneath the settee.

"Now, go see Larwi. She and the others will help you

escape before Father and Gavril notice we're up to anything. Irsa is in the drift yard. Gavril couldn't hold her."

Roan shook her head, the motion making her hair flutter from its loose braid. She didn't want to see Irsa. She didn't want the Witch of the Deep's help.

"I know Gavril told you that Irsa did this to trick you, but she didn't. Trust me, if you trust no one else. Gavril stole your voice from her and used it to give one of his followers legs. So he could lure your human out to sea."

Roan scrambled to the floor, trying to find the pen so she could scratch another note with it. She needed to know why. She needed to know what purpose this served. She needed to know how she could trust Irsa.

Fars took her hands and pulled her up onto her bent tail to meet her eyes. "There isn't time, Roan. They've already convinced him to rent a boat for tonight."

Roan opened her mouth to release a sound of panic, but nothing came out. She had to go. She had to get to Irsa. She had to save Jiro.

"I've written everything down for you." Fars pulled a folded piece of paper from the cushion on the sofa. "Go to Lawri. Let our sisters help you. Let Irsa help you."

EIGHTEEN

Irsa

It was *her* smile this time. It had been there one moment, in the front of Irsa's mind, radiant as it always was. And then it had faded, gone blurry, and vanished all together. Worn away and rubbed smooth like carved stone under water. Soon there would be nothing left of her. Only the holes where she had been. And then there would be nothing left of Irsa either, only the hate and loathing for herself and Tynan.

But before that. Before there was nothing left but darkness, Irsa would fight. She would fight and she would see Tynan and Gavril turned to nothing before her eyes.

"Mistress, Princess Roan has crossed our wards. She is alone."

"Let her in." Irsa didn't stop the flow of magic running from her fingers like a river into the warming dagger. She would finish this; she would finish them. Before they could hurt *her* daughters further.

"We are unsure if that is wise after Gavril's deception. She may have come here to—"

"I said, let her in!"

"Yes, Mistress."

They left her alone. The dagger burned hotter under her hands. Hot enough to make the water around it boil and the wood of the ship's deck smolder. It wasn't exactly the weapon she had wanted, but it would do for the task ahead of her. It would slice through the barrier and let her into Alon to finish this once and for all, magic intact. She'd prefer to have their fight out in the open ocean, where less people were likely to get hurt, but needs must. And what was a little more blood on her hands?

She felt the princess more than heard her when she entered the room. The soft hum of Roan's magic, so similar to *hers*, made Irsa's chest ache. Her fingers twitched to press into the bruising pain she felt beneath her breastbone. But she couldn't stop the flow of magic, not yet. Not until this was done.

"If you've come to finish me off, just do it already. Don't float there hemming and hawing about it. I've got things to do." When had she started sounding like the pit? When had that cold and anger seeped into her voice? Irsa couldn't remember anymore. Perhaps it had been while watching the princess throw back the gift she'd been given like it meant nothing. Like it hadn't cost Irsa two of the happiest years of her life. Or maybe it had been before, long before. Maybe it hadn't even come from the pit. Maybe it had come from Calypso. She shook herself. Not the time. Now was not the time to dredge up old hurts.

"Well? What do you want?" She jerked her head around to glare at Roan. The girl was still floating in the door, her hands clenched so hard around an envelope that the paper was beginning to wrinkle.

Roan took a breath, her shoulders rising with it, and then she nodded to herself. She closed the distance between herself and Irsa and held out the crumpled letter.

"I know you're new at this, but you don't bring letters to the people you plan to kill. You just kill them." Irsa didn't look at the envelope. She watched Roan's set expression. The girl knew what she was doing, knew what she wanted. Her green eyes were hard and sure, a gaze that was so similar, so familiar. Perhaps she'd been wrong about Roan. Perhaps she had more of her mother's fight in her than Irsa had originally thought.

Roan pushed the letter closer, practically stuffing it under Irsa's nose.

"Not taking no for an answer, I see." Irsa sighed, ending her connection to the dagger with a sizzle. She took the note, ripping it open and reading it over quickly. She stopped, frowning, the words not quite making sense, and started again from the top, mouthing the words along with her mind.

She had a choice to make—not that it was much of a choice at all. She could use Gavril's temporary distraction to go after Tynan when he was unprotected and unprepared. Or she could save Roan's soulmate. Vengeance or justice for *her*, those where Irsa's options. Irsa looked down at the dagger, still smoldering against the wood, and sighed. It had never really been a choice. Never would be one. If it were between making Tynan suffer and making sure *her* children were happy, Irsa would make the same decision. Every time.

"We have to go. Now."

Roan nodded eagerly, her hands making vague gestures in the water around her. Irsa didn't understand them, but she knew the sentiment behind them. They had to hurry.

"Did your sister know where they'd be taking him? There's a lot of sea between the beach where Gavril found you and here." Irsa moved to the work bench along the wall, pushing aside papers until she found a map. A human map. It wouldn't do them much good, but she might be able to pinpoint Jiro's location on it if she had a little of his soul-mate's blood.

Roan shook her head. She swam over to Irsa, looking at the map, her expression twisting into distress.

"All right then, we'll have to get as close as we can. They'll be moving, so . . . " Irsa wove her magic into the paper, watching as it rippled like water. "Give me your hand."

Roan looked at the outstretched fingers, a little frown on her lips.

"Roan, your hand. We don't have much time."

Roan huffed and pressed her palm to Irsa's. Irsa didn't give her any warning; she turned the girl's hand over, her fingers clasping Roan's wrist hard enough to bruise. She saw the fear flicker through those green eyes, but it was better this way. Better if Roan's magic rose up to defend her. It would make the blood more potent. The dagger flew from the floor, and Irsa used it to prick Roan's fingertip, then turned their hands so the blood fluttered through the water toward the map.

Roan's eyes were wide on the side of Irsa's face, but Irsa didn't look at her. She watched as the droplets turned stringy in the water, sinking for a long moment without purpose.

"Think of him," Irsa told Roan, glancing at her from the corner of her eyes.

It took a moment for Roan to conjure up whatever image she was using of Jiro, but when she did, the blood came alive. It moved through the water quicker, leaving a trail from her finger to a point just off the coast. Staining the map crimson on that spot, and then spreading west into the depths of the sea.

"We've got to get moving then. It looks like they're

headed our way." Irsa dropped Roan's wrist and went for the door without a glance back to make sure the princess was following her. It might actually be better if she weren't there at all, but Irsa wasn't going to fight her on it. "We'll catch the jet stream and go from there."

Roan nodded.

THE SUN WAS BRIGHT, blinding, when Irsa surfaced to search for the boat Jiro was on. It reflected off the water and right into her eyes, which took a moment to adjust to the sudden shift.

Roan smacked Irsa's shoulder and pointed. Irsa followed the gesture, and there on the horizon was a little boat. Only big enough for five people at most, a loud engine growling behind it as it went. A dingy, really, if Irsa remembered her human boat terms correctly.

"You stay here." Irsa started toward the boat.

Roan grabbed her wrist, giving it a sharp squeeze.

"Roan, we don't have time to argue! You stay here!" Irsa didn't wait for Roan to respond, her flippers flicking in the water as she lowered herself so just her head was above it. Keeping an eye on the boat, she made her way toward it. There were two people onboard: Jiro and a woman with black hair. Likely the one Gavril had given Roan's voice.

Irsa had just gotten close enough to the boat to be able to make out the figures when she noticed the mer swarming it. Just below the surface, a small army dove and wove beneath the wood, their magic crackling dangerously, making the water sparkle. The sea shifted, and the water grew rough. A whistle, and Irsa looked over at Roan to see the girl was pointing to the sky. Dark clouds rumbled, low and threatening, rolling in from the south.

Rain started, soft at first, then coming down in thick sheets. Gavril. That's where Gavril must have been. He was the only one who could brew a storm like that. The only one with enough power, outside of herself.

One of the mer from below grabbed the edge of the boat, pulling himself up onto its deck. Lightning caught the flash of a dagger.

Irsa floated, frozen, just above the water, watching it. Shell shocked at how this had all gone so horribly wrong. At how she'd put all of their lives in danger, Roan, and Fars, and this stupid human. She needed to . . . She needed to—

"Roan! No!"

The princess had taken off, swimming as fast as she could toward the boat, her red hair flowing behind her.

Irsa needed to protect Roan and stop the storm.

She ducked beneath the water, reaching within herself for the dark, writhing magic of the depths. She felt every creature from leagues away open their eyes, perk their fins up, and answer her call.

"Yes, Mistress?" a thousand voices rang through her mind.

"Protect the princess. Save the human. Stop those mer. I'll handle Gavril."

"Yes, Mistress." The creatures writhed and rose, bringing their darkness with them from the deepest parts of the oceans.

Her fins had already begun to push her to the south when she saw the first squid rise from the depths. Its tentacles reached for one of the mer on the outskirts and yanked it deeper, wrapping one long arm around the mer's neck and squeezing and squeezing. Irsa shook herself and reached within for her own magic to push herself farther, faster. She had to find Gavril. She had to stop the storm.

Gavril had found himself a seat on a buoy to watch the show, the light atop it flickering in and out as his magic interfered with whatever made it work. Beside him was Tynan, sprawled in a heap of long turquoise hair and fins.

Gavril saw her coming.

His magic leaped from his fingers where he was weaving the storm to strike at her in the water. A bolt of lightning sizzled a warning against her skin.

"Go home, Irsa! Go back to your little sea creatures!" Gavril's voice boomed through the thunder.

A tendril of violet magic reached from her, slithering over the current to grab at Gavril's wrist. To wrest the control of the storm from him. She could feel his connection to it humming there, just beneath his skin, like the current. Irsa gritted her teeth and pulled, the tentacle of magic tugging against her still battered body. But he wouldn't budge. And he laughed, loud like the waves during a tsunami.

"You think that's enough to stop me? I have the magic of the king of Alon. Do you know what that means, Irsa?" He jerked his wrist, yanking hard on the tentacle to whip her around in the water.

Bile rose, sharp and metallic, at the back of her throat, but she held on. She twisted and tightened her magic around his wrist, the force enough to bruise, giving it another firm yank. If she could just unseat him long enough to distract him, she could stop the storm. All she needed was one good tug to get him into the water with her, where she could reach him better. Where maybe one of her beasties could trap him.

"It means I have the power of every mer in Alon! Tynan never knew how to harness it, how to use it. He was weak, and now he's dead." Gavril shook off the hold she had on him, her violet magic slapping against the water, then lashed out with his own power. It sizzled and cracked like fire on wet wood, laced with the turquoise of Tynan's own power as it wrapped around her neck and squeezed, threatening to choke the life out of her.

Irsa took a breath, closed her eyes, and reached, not for the power within her but for the darkness that writhed around her. The depths would always rise to meet her, no matter where she was, so long as she called for them. So long as she gave them what they asked for in return, her memories of *her*. There would be nothing left after this fight, but it wouldn't matter then, because she'd have done what she promised herself she would.

Black, greasy magic rose up around her like oil on the tide. Less tentacle or fin, more an amorphous shape, a writhing mass that lurked where the ocean was at its deepest. Full of creatures no mer wanted to ever talk about. Of ancient things long forgotten. Krakens, and great eels, and things that had no name, no form, just darkness. Irsa's hand lifted to where Gavril's magic was tightening around her neck, making the skin bubble. She grabbed ahold of it and pulled, not even feeling as her palms turned raw and blistered. The blackness wriggled up her fins and tail, making its way over her to cover every inch. Turning her into what it needed her to be. Not a mer. A host.

Gavril gritted his teeth, his attention ripped away from the storm he was pushing toward Roan and Jiro, and focused solely on keeping his balance on the buoy. It was getting more and more slippery as the rain poured down around them, but the lightning was less directed now, less likely to strike Roan or Jiro.

"You can't do both," Irsa said, voice slightly strangled by the hold he still had on her neck. It was making breathing hard, but she supposed she didn't need to breathe for too much longer. Just long enough to take Gavril with her.

"You can't kill that human and fight me. You have to make a choice." And then she laughed, high and manic.

He lashed out with another rope of his own sizzling magic, grabbing for her wrist. What he hoped to accomplish, she didn't know, nor did she care. Irsa's smile was a knife slash across her face. Blood welled up in the back of her throat. She'd die soon. This would be her last battle. More memories of *her* flashed through her mind, beautiful and ethereal, each fading just as quickly as they'd come.

Irsa met Gavril's eyes through her swimming vision. Saw the look of strain on his face. He was losing. What power he had wouldn't be enough; it would never be enough. Because he wasn't willing to make the sacrifices she was. Because he had more to lose than she did. What did Irsa have left? A few battered memories? Even those were quickly fading. What was it she'd been fighting for anyway . . .

Gavril lunged, perhaps thinking to strangle her himself, his hands outstretched and buzzing with the power of an eel.

A mistake. A foolish, foolish mistake. A lethal mistake.

It barely even took a thought on her part. Just the faintest nudge into the black with her will.

The shadows sharpened into a blade, catching Gavril mid-leap and burying into his middle. He made a choking sound, like a fish out of water, and then went still. Irsa looked at him, looked at his lifeless eyes, and let out a breath. With a flick of her wrist, she called the shadows back, and they dropped him with a splash into the water, blood pooling around them. Her hands caught for a moment on the black scales that clung now to her arms.

No. There would be time to worry about how the magic had changed her later.

The seas didn't calm. Gavril had used magic to call the

storm, but it wasn't magic in and of itself. It was nature. Even if she'd wanted to, even with all the powers of the Deep, she couldn't stop it.

"Irsa! Help me!" Roan screamed.

The boat was in ruins when Irsa turned to see what Roan was screaming about. The water was red with blood. But Roan was there. Roan, who was . . . Who had she been again? Irsa shook herself. Roan was holding the unconscious human in her arms, trying to get him to safety as the waves lashed against her.

"Take the king to his children," Irsa said to an anglerfish lingering just below the surface. A small act of mercy. A nod to . . . to someone. Someone who had loved her . . . once. "He should have a proper burial."

"Yes, Mistress."

With the writhing shadows of the Deep still darkening her fins, Irsa pushed herself toward the wreckage and looped one of Jiro's arms over her shoulders.

NINETEEN

Roan

———

He wasn't bleeding. There was so much blood, but none of it was his. Roan thanked Amiphrite for that. Her fin flicked harder toward the shore. She needed to get him to land, to check his breathing, to make sure he was all right.

"He's fine," Irsa said, soft but confident, from where she swam alongside Roan. Roan could hardly look at her now. The witch had changed. Black scales clinging to her arms and cheeks, eyes without whites, and fingers more like talons than anything else, so sharp Roan half feared they'd tear the delicate skin on Jiro's ribs. But still, Irsa was helping her. "It's probably just the shock."

"He . . . he saw my fins," Roan whispered, still amazed that she could. Amazed that the moment Sabrina had regained her fins, the voice had been ripped from her throat and returned to Roan. "Will Sabrina be all right?"

"Who?"

"The one Gavril gave my voice to. She was . . . There was a lot of blood."

"I don't know. I don't know what magic he used to give her legs." Irsa shrugged, unconcerned. She didn't seem to care what became of the people who had swum against her, and Roan wasn't sure what that meant. Did that mean Irsa was evil? She looked the part, but that didn't mean much of anything, Roan was coming to realize. Roan pushed the thought aside in favor of turning Jiro onto his side in the sand in case he needed to cough up water. "Now what?"

Irsa stretched her fin out on the sand. There was blood dribbling from the corner of her mouth, but she didn't seem like she was in pain at all, in spite of the darkness that clung to her. "Now what, what?"

"What do I do now?" Roan rubbed Jiro's back, wishing she had an umbrella to shield him from the rain as it kept coming down in sheets. She felt his back move beneath her hand. At least he was breathing.

Irsa tilted her head at her and shrugged. "Whatever you want, I guess. Gavril is dead. Your father is dead. Fars will take the throne."

"Father is dead?" It hurt. It hurt like heartbreak all over again. Like her chest seizing up.

"Yes. He is." Irsa said it like she didn't care. Like it didn't matter. And Roan supposed, to her, it didn't. After all, Irsa had gotten what she'd wanted, hadn't she? Vengeance on the man who'd taken from her what she loved the most. Roan supposed she couldn't be angry at her for this callousness.

Still, Irsa gave her time. They sat in silence, the rain running in thick rivers down her fins, as Roan tried to breathe through the pain of grief.

"What do you want to do?" Irsa's voice was so soft, Roan almost didn't hear it over the fall of droplets on the sand.

"What?"

"I said, what do you want to do, Roan? Do you want to go back to your life in Alon? Or do you want to go back to your life with Jiro?" The blood that had been at the corner of Irsa's mouth had started to dribble softly down her chin.

"Are you dying?"

"Does it matter?"

"Yes." Roan wasn't sure why, but it did. She didn't want to lose anyone else. Even if that someone was evil.

"Don't change the subject. What do you want to do?" Irsa coughed softly into her fist, then dropped it to the sand before Roan could see if there was blood coating her palm. "I can make you human again, if that's what you want."

"What will it cost me?"

"It didn't really cost you anything last time."

"My voice."

Irsa shook her head. "That was a precaution. To protect you and keep you from exposing yourself."

Roan looked out at the water, frowning. That didn't make sense. Magic like that had a price. It had—"What did it cost *you*?"

"Nothing I wasn't giving up anyway." Irsa's eyes had drifted out to the open ocean, which was slowly calming. She didn't seem to want to look at Roan anymore, and Roan wasn't sure why.

Nothing she wasn't giving up anyway.

"Irsa."

"I gave up memories. Two years of them. And if I do this for you now, I'll give up the rest of them. Everything I've ever known, every person I've ever met, every day I've ever lived." Irsa's voice was soft, but she'd lifted her hands and begun to weave the magic, not even waiting for Roan to confirm that was what she wanted. It was, of course it was.

Of course she wanted to be human, to live with Jiro, to discover new things. But not at the cost of someone else's life.

"Please don't do this. You . . . you don't have to do this." Tears tightened Roan's throat. Irsa wasn't going to give her a choice. She could feel it. Irsa had decided for her. But maybe . . . maybe she could make her stop.

"I do."

"Why?"

"For her."

"Her?" Roan's throat clenched around the word. She didn't want to ask, but she thought she already knew. Mother. Irsa had given up her memories for Mother. For Aislin. "Her who?"

"I don't remember." Irsa hadn't stopped weaving the magic. It was settling over Roan's fin like a net, slowly growing tighter and tighter.

"Why?! You don't even remember her name! You don't owe her this!" Roan choked on the words, the tears rolling down her face in hot streams to contrast the cool rain slowing above them.

"You're right. I don't remember her name." Irsa nodded as if in confirmation, but her tone was devoid of any emotion. She seemed strangely detached from the fact that she couldn't even remember the name of the person she'd sold her soul for. "And after this . . . " She took a breath as if to steady herself. "Well, after this, I won't remember mine either."

"Please. No." Weak, her words were weak. Lost to the pain of the net of magic cutting her open. Slicing through her tail, scraping off her scales, and rearranging her bones. There was blood. So much blood on the sand. She'd never noticed the blood before, likely because the water had been so dark. But it coated the sand, making it thick and sticky like paste beneath her.

"It's all right now, Roan. It'll be all right." Irsa shushed her gently, one hand reaching out to guide her to lay back in the sand.

"Please." She didn't want this. Not at the cost of another person's memories. Not at the cost of everything that made another person who they were.

"This is how it was always going to end." Irsa coughed, blood dribbling down to her neck when her hands were too busy to catch it. She was going to die; Roan was sure of it. And her last act would be to give up everything for a mer she hardly knew. "This was the only way it ever could."

And then Roan lost herself to the pain of her tail being whittled down and reformed into human legs. She screamed. She screamed so loud, it left her throat tasting like bile and the sharp metallic bite of blood. And when she finally came back to herself, when she finally opened her eyes, the rain had stopped. The moon was peeking from behind soft, fluffy clouds. And the space where the sea witch had been was empty. Not even a trail left where she'd dragged herself back down to the water.

All that was left was the man beside her, slowly coming back to consciousness, and the pile of scales Irsa's magic had peeled away.

Epilogue - Roan

The sand dug into her knees through her soft nightgown, cold and hard. The waves crashed in a low rumble against the shore. Roan looked up at the moon, the stars twinkling around it, and then lowered her gaze back to the little altar Jiro had made for her along the beach. Their beach. Their altar. Their home. Just close enough to Alon to see her sisters but not so far from the rest of the world that they couldn't continue their research when called upon.

"Please, Amiphrite," she whispered, her fingers fisting in the sand. "Please take care of them."

"Roan? What are you doing, my love? It's late." Jiro's voice was soft, a smile softening the edges, like he already knew the answer.

Roan looked up from the statue he'd gotten Milo to carve for her of Amiphrite. Or what Roan imagined Amiphrite might look like. It looked remarkably similar to a witch who, some years ago, had given everything up so Roan could be happy. She smiled at him, sadness lingering below the edges, humming through her veins.

"Just praying to the sea goddess that they'll find one another again." She'd also asked Amiphrite to look fondly upon her child, and to bless them with a safe delivery, but Jiro didn't need to know about that . . . yet.

"Who?"

"Aislin and Irsa." The names still stung her throat like sea nettles, making her eyes burn with the pain. So close. She'd been so close to knowing the woman who had loved her mother. And she had slipped through her fingers. In the end, she'd lost them both. "I hope when they find each other again, things are different."

Jiro came to kneel beside her, giving a bow to the statue just as she had before. The understanding she saw behind his glasses made her heart skip. But now was not the time for that.

Roan trailed her fingers through the sea water in the bowl she'd scooped from the tides, feeling the softness of the sand at the bottom. "I pray the world is kinder to them next time. They deserve happiness."

"They do." Jiro nodded. "And you deserve sleep. Come on, we have a big day of research ahead of us. We don't want Milo to beat us to that paper on ocean mythology, do we?"

"No, we don't." Roan laughed, letting him help her to her feet after one last bow to Amiphrite. She smiled down at the little altar, gave it one last nod, and let Jiro lead her away. Back home.

The sand dug into her knees through her soft nightgown, cold and hard. The waves crashed in a low rumble against the shore. Roan looked up at the moon, the stars twinkling around it, and then lowered her gaze back to the little alter Jiro had made for her along the beach. Their beach. Their alter. Their home. Just close enough to Alon to see her sisters, but not so far from the rest of the world that they couldn't continue their research when called upon.

"Please Amiphrite," she whispered, her fingers fisting in the sand. "Please take care of them."

"Roan? What are you doing, my love? It's late." Jiro's voice was soft, a smile softening the edges, like he already knew the answer.

Roan looked up from the statue he'd gotten Milo to carve for her of Amiphrite. Or what Roan imagined Amiphrite might look like. It looked remarkably similar to a witch who some years ago had given everything up so Roan could be happy. She smiled at him, sadness lingering below the edges of it, humming through her veins.

"Just praying to the sea goddess that they'll find one another again." She'd also asked Amiphrite to look fondly upon her child, and bless them with a safe delivery, but Jiro didn't need to know about that... yet.

"Who?"

"Aislin and Irsa." The names still stung her throat like sea nettles, making her eyes burn with the pain. So close. She'd been so close to knowing the woman who had loved her mother. And it had slipped through her fingers. In the end, she'd lost them both. "I hope when they find each other again things are different."

Jiro came to kneel beside her, giving a bow to the statue just as she had before. The understanding she saw behind his glasses made her heart skip. But now was not the time for that.

Roan trailed her fingers through the sea water in the bowl she'd scooped from the tides, feeling the softness of the sand at the bottom. "I pray the world is kinder to them next time. They deserve happiness."

"They do." Jiro nodded. "And you deserve sleep. Come on, we have a big day of research ahead of us. We don't want Milo to beat us to that paper on ocean mythology. Do we?"

"No, we don't." Roan laughed, letting him help her to her feet after one last bow to Amiphrite. She smiled down at the little alter, gave it one last nod, and let Jiro lead her away. Back home.

Acknowledgments

First off, thank you—the reader—for reading this continuation of Irsa's story. If you read the first book when it came out, I know you had a bit of a wait, and I really appreciate you hanging in there. I hope you'll drop a review on Good-Reads to let me know what you think.

For those of you who may feel unsatisfied with the ending (if you're returning readers you should know me well enough by now) I want to let you know that there is still one more book in Irsa's story. And the publishing date is next year! So, if all things go according to plan you won't have too long to wait.

Next, I'd like the thank my small hoard of beta-readers. You guys gave some excellent insight, and I really appreciate all of your hard work. And my editor Meg for turning this into a story worth reading.

And last but certainly not least, thank you to my writing community. Particularly, Tiss, Elle, and Jasmine who I have known for near a decade now—without you there would be no Lou. And to my new friends, Candace, Melanie, Nancy, and Tanya for being supportive and awesome.

About the Author

Born and raised in a small town near the Chesapeake Bay, Lou Wilham grew up on a steady diet of fiction, arts and crafts, and Old Bay. After years of absorbing everything, there was to absorb of fiction, fantasy, and sci-fi she's left with a serious writing/drawing habit that just won't quit. These days, she spends much of her time writing, drawing, and chasing a very short Basset Hound named Sherlock.

When not, daydreaming up new characters to write and draw she can be found crocheting, making cute bookmarks, and binge-watching whatever happens to catch her eye.

Learn more about Lou and her future projects on her website: http://louinprogress.com/ or join her mailing list at: http://subscribepage.com/mailermailer

facebook.com/LouWilham

instagram.com/lou.wilham

More Books You'll Love

If you enjoyed this story,
please consider leaving a review.

Then check out more books from
Midnight Tide Publishing!

The Rose and the Claw by Nancy O'Toole

A woman on a mission...

Rose Gardner never thought she'd leave the small town of West Ridge. But when her husband dies at war, she must return his arms to his place of birth to set his spirit to rest. After traveling into enemy territory, Rose falls into a trap. Held captive in an enchanted manor, she finds herself face to face with a beast who is equally horrifying and kind. Will she manage to complete her quest or be pulled in by the secrets of the manor?

A man haunted by his past...

Trapped within his own home and in the body of a hideous beast, Kris never wanted to share his prison with another. As much as Rose may draw him in with her beauty and stubborn strength, he knows she must escape before the next full moon. After all, he remembers all too well what happened to the previous caretaker.

The dead won't let him forget the blood on his hands.

Available on
8.4.21

Ephesus by Christis Christie

As a soul lost before it could live, Ephesus was gifted a special role — he must collect the dead.

Ephesus has known no other existence than reaping souls, experiencing life only from the shadows. Remaining separate was easy, until the day he meets a unique little girl with an ability she should not possess.

But can friendships be nurtured when life and death aren't meant to mingle beyond the point of passing? Ephesus must navigate the world fulfilling his purpose while also balancing his newfound curiosity of the girl's life. However, when a threat arises, will it mean their ruin?

Available October 20

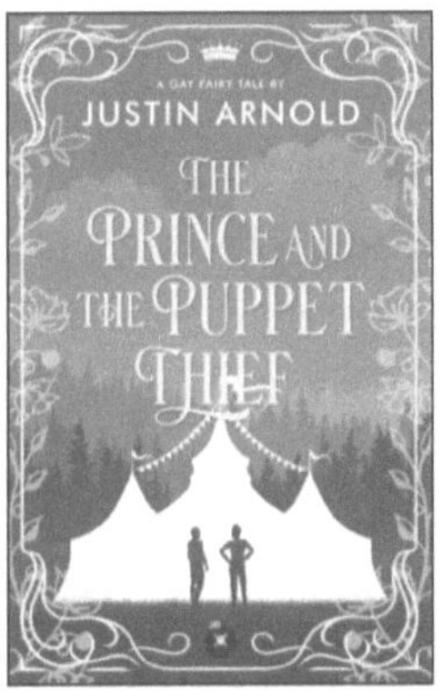

The Prince and the Puppet Thief by Justin Arnold

Welcome to the kingdom where princes kiss thieves, princesses dance with their handmaids at midnight, and non-binary magicians see to it that everyone gets their happy-ever-after.

17-year-old Simon The Squirm has spent his life on the run- and he hates it. Breaking the law gives him anxiety, and he always forgets to carry a weapon. Being the son of the 2nd most feared villain in the kingdom has never been easy, but when an ill-conceived plan to steal the Lost Princess's slippers lands him in the dungeon, he makes up his mind to take the first opportunity at freedom.

Prince Marco isn't convinced he's the one to rescue the

lost Princess Isobel. Sure, he's a handsome and brave royal straight out of a fairy tale- but that doesn't mean he's ready to fall for the first damsel in distress who sends out an S.O.S. When he finds himself smitten with the sarcastic (if bumbling) Simon, a scheme is hatched to save both of them from a not-so-happily-ever-after.

The mission is simple: Simon must go in Marco's place to rescue the princess and defeat the wicked magician who stole her. But when it becomes clear that Princess Isobel would rather be saved by her handmaid, Prince Marco and Simon might just end up rescuing each other instead.

Perfect for fans of *The Two Princes* podcast and Sonan Chainani, *The Prince And The Puppet Thief* is a hilarious and swoon-worthy fairy tale rom-com by and for the LGBT community.

Available August 18

The P.A.N. by Jenny Hickman

Since her parents were killed, Vivienne has always felt ungrounded, shuffled through the foster care system. Just when liberation finally seems possible—days before her eighteenth birthday—Vivienne is hospitalized with symptoms no one can explain.

The doctors may be puzzled, but Deacon, her mysterious new friend, claims she has an active Nevergene. His far-fetched diagnosis comes with a warning: she is about to become an involuntary test subject for Humanitarian Organization for Order and Knowledge—or HOOK. Vivienne can either escape to Neverland's Kensington

Academy and learn to fly (Did he really just say fly?) or risk sticking around to become a human lab rat. But accepting a place among The PAN means Vivienne must abandon her life and foster family to safeguard their secrets and hide in Neverland's shadows… forever.

Available Now

Credits

Seaweed Free Icon made by smalllikeart from
www.flaticon.com/authors/smalllikeart

www.ingramcontent.com/pod-product-compliance
Lightning Source LLC
Chambersburg PA
CBHW021149190726

48288CB00008B/2898